BRON

REAPER-Patriots

Book TWENTY-SIX

Mary Kennedy

INSATIABLE INK.

This book is a work of fiction. The names, characters, places, and incidents are products of the writer's imagination or have been used fictitiously and are not to be constructed as real. Any resemblance to persons, living or dead, actual events, locales, or organizations is entirely coincidental.

Editing provided by: pccProofreading

MAP of Belle Fleur and Cottage Assignments

Readers – if you're like me – you're very visual – I hope this map helps as you're reading.

Readers – you'll notice some changes on the map to make it clearer and easier to read. The characters have the same cottage numbers, it just looks different. I've also added a guide to the families and books at the back. I hope you find these resources helpful.

G1-8 = Garçonnière
Big House = Belle Fleur – main house of Matthew and Irene Robicheaux, with George & Mary
The Grove – where BBQ's, picnics, and family gatherings take place

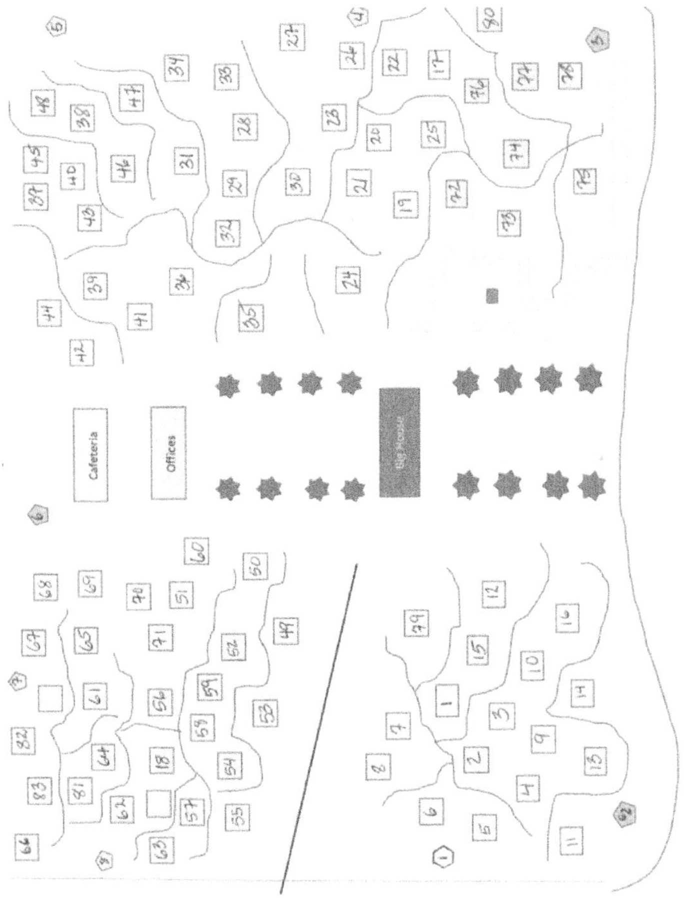

COTTAGE Assignments

1	Miller & Kari	31	Hawk & Keegan	61	Hunter & Megan	83	
2	Alec & Lissa	32	Eagle & Tinley	62	Cam & Kate	84	
3	Gabe & Tori	33	Ace & Charlie	63	Jax & Ellie	85	
4	Gaspar & Alex	34	Razor & Bella	64	Adam & Jane	86	
5	Raphael & Savannah	35	Tango & Taylor	65	Ben & Harper	87	
6	Baptiste & Rose	36	Gunner & Darby	66	Carl & Georgie	88	
7	Antoine & Ella	37	Ghost & Grace	67	Striker & Violet	88	
8	Ivan & Sophia	38	Zulu & Gabi	68	Molly & Asia	89	
9	Tristan & Emma	39	Doc & Bree	G1	Hiro & Winter	90	
10	Luc & Montana	40	Paul & Elizabeth	G2	Bron	91	
11	King & Claire	41	Luke & Ajei	G3	Fitch	92	
12	Sly & Suzette	42	Fitz & Zoe	G4	Eric & Sophia Ann	93	
13	Rory & Piper	43	RJ & Celia	69	Kiel & Liz	94	
14	O'Hara & Lucia	44	Carter & Ani	70	Joseph & Julia	95	
15	Titus & Olivia	45	Bull & Lily	71	Wes & Virginia	96	
16	Max & Riley	46	Trev & Ashley	72	Dalton & Calla	97	
17	Stone & Bronwyn	47	Whiskey & Kat	73	Nathan & Katrina	98	
18	Jazz & Gray	48	Tailor & Lena	74	Keith & Susie	99	
19	Vince & Ally	49	Angel & Mary	75	Marc & Ela	100	
20	Phoenix & Raven	50	Bryce & Ivy	76	Jake & Claudette	101	
21	Noah & Tru	51	Wilson & Sara	77	Frank & Lane	102	
22	Griff & Amanda	52	Mac & Rachelle	78	Ian & Aspen	103	
23	Gibbie & Dhara	53	Nine & Erin	79	Doug & Miguel	104	
24	Blade & Suzette	54	Clay & Adele	80	Dom & Leightyn	105	
25	Skull & Avery	55	Trak & Lauren	G5	Parker & Dani	106	
26	Axel & Cait	56	Lars & Jessica	G6	Michael	107	
27	Sniff & Lucy	57	Ian & Faith	G7	Sean & Shay	108	
28	Noa & Kelsey	58	Zeke & Noelle	G8	Ryan & Paige	109	
29	Eli & Jane	59	Jean & Ro	81	Aiden & Brit	110	
30	Grant & Evie	60	Dexter & Marie	82			

CHAPTER ONE

Bron looked up at his mother, rolling his eyes as he watched her flirt with the man standing behind them in the grocery store line. It was bad enough that she had dinner with Principal Jaguari last week. Now she's laughing at this man's stupid jokes and touching his arm.

He wasn't anything special. He looked tall, and he was Hispanic which seemed to be his mother's preference in men. But what if he was married? Or he could be a kidnapper!

"Mom," he said, tugging her arm. "Mom, it's your turn."

"Okay, baby. You put the things on the belt, and I'll pay. Let me finish talking to this nice man." She turned back to the man behind her, and Bron just rolled his eyes again. He caught the man handing his mother a slip of paper, no doubt with his phone number on it. Paying for the groceries, she tucked it in her purse and left the grocery store.

He helped his mother set the groceries in the trunk of the car and then got in and buckled himself into the seat. Staring out the window, he noticed the man waving at his mother.

"Why are you so quiet?" she asked.

"Because," he said in a frustrated tone. "You were flirting with that man, and it's gross! You went out with Principal Jaguari last week. Now this stranger is giving you his phone number."

"Baby, I'm still a young, attractive woman, and I don't want to die alone. You'll be off to college in a few years, and I'll be stuck here all by myself. I just want someone to do adult things with, Bron. Go to movies, maybe have dinner, that's all."

"Why don't you just call my dad? I'd like to see him, get to know him," he said with a pleading tone. Amara Jones looked at her son, her heart cracking for the need she saw in his face.

"Baby, I know you want to meet your dad, but he just never wanted kids. He was a good man. He treated me well, and we were happy, but when I got pregnant with you, he just left. I'm not mad about it. I knew that if it happened, he would leave me."

"Well, then he wasn't a very good man," said Bron.

"Don't say that, Bron. He was. I promise. I loved your daddy, but I loved you more and wasn't willing to give you up. I just want to find a nice man to spend some adult time with. Like I said, go to movies, dinners, that sort of thing."

"I'd go with you," he said sweetly to his mother.

His pleading tone almost made Amara want to tell him why she really needed a man, but that would come soon enough. Her handsome son would have women wanting his body sooner rather than later. With his creamy, latte-colored skin, and thick, wavy black hair, he was a beautiful combination of his father's Hispanic-European background and her African background.

Her own skin was nearly his color, but there was something about Bron's that just glowed. Where her hair had the wiry curls of her African heritage, his had waves of jet-black creole hair. His eyes were a light hazel, his lips full and pouty. He was beautiful, and he was her son.

"Baby, I know you'd go with me, and I love going to the movies and dinners with you. Sometimes, though, adults need other adults to spend time with."

"For sex?" he asked. Amara wanted to choke, but she held her composure and smiled at her son.

"Sometimes. It doesn't always end up that way. When you're older, you'll get a feeling in your stomach and in your chest when you want to be intimate with a woman. It's not something to take lightly, Bron. There are consequences for every action, and you need to learn that the consequences of unprotected sex could be a child. You'll have those feelings soon enough."

"I won't," he said defiantly.

"Bron, I know you think you won't, but you will. It's normal. It's natural, and it's beautiful. You just have to be sure that the young woman is deserving of you. Some girls aren't very nice."

"I already know that," he said casually. Amara raised her eyes, hoping that at twelve, some girl wasn't offering her body to him. "Holly Baldwin acts like she likes me when she wants to cheat on a test, but then when we're at recess, she calls me names."

"What kind of names, baby?"

"Half-breed. Mixed-breed. Zebra. It's all stupid stuff. There's lots of kids at school who have different looking parents. She's just blonde with blue eyes and thinks she's perfect."

"Well, she's not perfect. No one is, but one day you'll find someone that's perfect for you."

Bron helped his mother with the groceries, thinking about their conversation. He didn't want his mother to be alone, especially when he left for college or the Marine Corps. He hadn't decided which. As he put away the last of the items, he turned to his mother.

"Hey, Mom? I think it's okay if you want to call that guy from the store. I want you to be happy." She smiled at her son, hugging him tightly to her chest, kissing the top of his head.

"I have the night shift at the nursing home tonight. I'm going to go lay down for a nap, and then I'll call him to see if he wants to meet for dinner this week. Do you want me to call Mrs. Garr for you tonight?"

"No," he said, shaking his head. "I'll be okay, Mom. She's right next door if I need her, but I usually fall asleep, so I'm good."

"Okay, baby."

Amara watched her son go into their backyard, picking up his bat and ball, and hitting balls into the netting they'd stretched across the back of the fence. About once a month, he would ask about his father, and once a month, she had to lie. Antonio Gardella was someone she'd slept with a dozen times. He was sexy, hot as all get out, suave, and damn good in bed.

They'd spent about a month together, screwing like rabbits, and then one morning, he said he was moving on. His sister lived in Miami, and he was headed down there to work in her husband's business. They'd made no promises to one another. She had no hold on him whatsoever.

Amara shrugged, kissed him goodbye, and discovered she was pregnant exactly four weeks later. She never bothered to try and find him. She knew the score. He didn't want to be tied down. He didn't want children, and she wasn't about to end the life growing inside her.

It was just her and Bron. Her little man, growing too fast for his own good. As a nurse, she earned a decent living and was able to buy the little house they lived in and provide for her son. She had a good running vehicle and money for extras if she needed it. She was fine with it just being the two of them.

She called grocery store man, who turned out to have a real name, Aldrich Bennett. They dated for four months, married, and divorced five years later. There wasn't any cheating or hitting or anything scandalous. They were just done.

Four weeks before Bron graduated from high school, Amara accepted a dinner invitation from his old middle-school principal, Hector Jaguari. They married a year later, and during Bron's second deployment in the Marine Corps, they divorced.

It would be ten years later before she married again. It seemed old news to Bron when she would announce a new man in her life. He loved his mother, but her ability to detect long-term partners was not exactly stellar. Of course, neither was his.

"Lora, you knew that I might be deployed when we married, baby. This isn't something that's negotiable. It's my job. When the Marine Corps says 'go,' I have to go! And right now, I have to go."

"We just got married, Bron! I've been your wife for less than two months, and now you're telling me you're leaving me for at least six months. What kind of marriage is that? Am I supposed to stay here and not have sex while I'm waiting for you? Am I supposed to play bridge with the other Marine wives?"

Bron's face darkened as he stared at Lora from across the room. He shoved the stack of t-shirts into his duffel and looked down, then back up at her. Yea, he expected her to have no sex.

"Just what the fuck do you think I'm going to be doing, Lora? I'm with a platoon of Marines fighting a war. Do you think we're fucking each other?"

"There are women, Bron. I know there are. Nurses, female military members, hell, even the Afghan women are offering themselves up. I've seen the stories. I know your appetite, and I know you like sex a lot. I know you like it rough, too. I bet some of those female Marines don't mind giving it to you rough."

"Not cool, Lora. I like sex a lot with my wife, not other women. Don't disrespect me that way. I don't fuck around, and I don't appreciate you insinuating that I do. I'm asking you, as my wife, to wait for me to return. Please don't do anything stupid. I'll call; I'll e-mail; I'll do everything I can to stay in touch with you, but MARSOC is different."

She sat on the edge of the bed, and Bron knelt in front of her, his big palms flat on her thighs. Her smooth skin felt amazing beneath his hands. They'd made love last night and again this morning, but damn if he didn't want her again in spite of her childlike outburst.

"I'll be back, Lora, I promise. There are a hundred other wives in the same boat. Get to know them. Support one another. Hell, you've got a full-time job, maybe work some extra shifts and put the money aside. By the time I get back with my overseas pay and your extra, we could buy a house."

She pushed him back, standing and leaving the bedroom. Bron secured the duffel and grabbed the rest of his gear.

"I have to go. I love you," he said, leaning down for a kiss. She turned her cheek away, and he could only shake his head. "Fitch is outside. I'll call when I can."

He left their small apartment, hoping she'd follow him outside, but she didn't. She didn't call him while they waited for their transport. She didn't respond to his text messages, and the first eight times he called, she didn't answer. He was miserable, but more than that, he was pissed off.

But nothing compared to when he returned. She wasn't at the base to greet him with all the other wives. There was no one running to leap into his arms. Instead, he found her standing in the middle of their living room, everything she owned already packed in her car.

"What the hell, Lora?" he said, looking around. "I guess your idea of welcoming me home and mine are two very different things."

"The papers are on the table, Bron. There's nothing to fight over, no property, no kids. Just sign them. This is simple. Just sign the papers, and we'll be done. We can both move on. I need to move on and have a life for myself."

He wanted to argue, wanted to scream and yell, and try to convince her to stay, but something was holding him back. The woman he'd met and married in less than two months wasn't who he thought. That made sense, considering how fast he'd rushed into it.

I guess that apple doesn't fall all that far, does it?

Maybe he didn't want to ask her to stay. He'd been overseas six months, and in that time, he had to chase her down when he wanted to speak to her or see her on video chat. She'd not initiated one e-mail, only responding in a few sentences to his multi-paragraph messages. She was right. They needed to move on.

Walking toward the table, he grabbed the pen, scribbled his name, and handed her the paperwork.

"Enjoy your life, Lora, but don't ever think you're coming back into mine." She looked as though she wanted to say something but instead turned and walked out, leaving Bron alone in his apartment.

Bron dropped his bags in their, his bedroom, showered, changed his clothes, and texted his friend, Fitch, to meet for a beer. By the time he hit the bar, Fitch was already three beers in.

"How long have you been here?" asked Bron.

"Twenty minutes," he growled. "Debbie left me."

"No shit," said Bron with a harumph. "Lora left me. Signed the fucking papers for her and everything."

"Debbie was pissed because I was fucking Tamara before I left."

"Dude, she was her best friend," said Bron, shaking his head. "Didn't it occur to you that they might talk? Maybe compare notes?" Fitch just shrugged as the men just drank, staring at the bar.

"I might ask Tamara to come over tonight," grinned Fitch. "I need to fuck something, and you're not getting any prettier."

"You're a crazy fucker, Fitch. I'm done. There won't be another marriage for me. I don't want to be my mom, already on number three, thinking there might be a number four. Nope. I got about ten years left, and then I'm out. Speaking of which, I ran into Nine and their team on our last day over there."

"No shit! How the hell are they doing? I've heard nothing but good things about their team."

"Yea, same. They're growing, brother. He told me to reach out when we got close, and I'll be honest, that's all I can think about right now."

"Well, if you go, I go." Bron nodded, grinning at his friend.

"Semper fi, asshole."

CHAPTER TWO

Bron had never enjoyed a mission so much in his entire career. Helping to keep Lane Quinn safe while escorting her and Frank Robicheaux across the country was the most fun he'd had in years. Plus, she was cool as shit, and Frank was one badass fucker. Like all the Robicheauxs, he was a big bastard with unsettling eyes that seemed to bore through you.

To top it off, he and Fitch met Rory Baine. *The* Rory Baine. Plus, Alec Robicheaux and Tailor Bongard. Legends. By the time they returned to southern California, both men were ready to turn in their retirement papers. RP was where they wanted to be.

Bron smiled as Dominic Quinn hugged his wife, their first dance as husband and wife in front of their friends and family. Beside them were Skull and Avery, also dancing their first dance. Both men deserved happiness, and damn sure both women did as well. But he was alone and seeing all the happy couples wasn't helping his mood. He'd resigned himself to the fact that he'd remain a bachelor, yet something about watching all this wedded bliss was tugging at his heart.

Earlier that morning, before the weddings, Hiro walked toward Bron with a strange look on his face. He didn't know him well, but he knew enough to know that if he had a serious expression, there was something wrong or suspicious.

"What's up, brother?"

"There's someone sending e-mail messages to you that are routed through your old military e-mail. She says she knows you and needs your help."

"Knows me? She? Who is it?" he asked.

"She signed them Lora Jones."

"Fuck."

"What? Who is she? Should I delete them?" asked Hiro.

"No. I'll answer them later. She's my ex-wife."

His fucking ex-wife. It had been ten years since he'd seen her face or heard her name. The day she walked out of their apartment, it was as if she'd dropped off the face of the planet. He tried to call and forward her mail, but she changed her phone number. Her parents were dead. She had no siblings, so he simply put it all in a big plastic bin. He held that mail for almost three years before he finally burned every last envelope.

Sitting there watching all the happy couples dancing was not doing anything for his quickly souring mood. He'd been joyful once upon a time. Danced with his wife, thinking this would be the beginning of their happily ever after.

They'd met at a holiday charity drive for service members and their children. Filling food baskets for enlisted men and their families, some who were living at poverty level, was something he was passionate about.

Standing on the other side of the room, she was filling bags with vegetables. She'd smiled at him several times, and finally, during lunch, he walked over and introduced himself. By that night, they were fucking like wildcats. She didn't leave his bed the entire weekend. Two months later, they were already talking about getting married. Two months after that, he was deployed. Six months after that, the bitch left him.

He'd heard through the grapevine after their divorce, that Lora spent a lot of time volunteering at veteran charities in hopes of meeting a spec ops guy. He should have seen that one coming.

He saw Mama Irene walking toward him and squirmed in his seat. He wondered if she had some young woman on the other side of the dance floor waiting for him. He did not have the temperament for this right now. She'd been wonderful to him and Fitch, welcoming them with open arms as another 'son' in her family, but he was not into the whole match-making game.

"Hi, baby," she said sweetly.

"Evening, Mama Irene. Another beautiful event," he said, trying to sound cheerful. She patted his hand, then leaned down and kissed his cheek.

"Don't worry, baby. Love comes to those who wait. She wasn't the woman intended for you. That one will come soon enough. Until then, try to enjoy what you've been given." She kissed his other cheek, leaving him with his thoughts. Seeing a group of young women seated at a table, he downed his beer and stood up.

"I'm done fucking waiting."

He swallowed the last drops of the beer and walked by one of the three bars, grabbing a bottle of whiskey. Approaching the table, he realized that some of the women had the telltale looks of Robicheauxs. He didn't think they were young enough to be daughters or granddaughters, but he damn sure didn't want his dick cut off. Instead, he asked two other women if they wanted to join him.

"Well, hello there," smiled the first woman.

"Hi," he grinned. "I'm Bron Jones."

"I know," said the second woman. "Aunt Irene told me."

"Oh, you're a Robicheaux cousin?" he asked.

"Baby, we're all related somehow. We're fourth cousins by marriage, but it doesn't matter in this family. We get invited. I'm Elena, and this is my sister, Veda."

"Nice to meet you both. Care to join me for a drink in the gardens?" he grinned. The girls giggled, and Bron panicked, wondering how old they were. "Hey, you're both over twenty-one, right?"

"Yea, baby, we're both over twenty-one. Let's go," said Veda, grabbing his hand.

He chugged the whiskey, feeling the burn of the liquid on his throat. It was a satisfying pain for just a moment, then it stilled, and he chugged again. His head started to spin, but he didn't give a fuck. He needed to forget. The two women pulled him toward the gardens, finally stopping near a stone bench between the shrubs of the maze. He took another swig, the women blurry versions of themselves.

"Have a seat, honey," said Elena.

She shoved him to the bench, and he was happy for the solid seat. Watching the two women, they both removed their panties, laying them beside him. Veda stood on the bench, her legs on either side of his thighs. She lifted the skirt of her dress, gripping his hair and guiding his mouth to her as she straddled his face.

"Fuck yea," he slurred. He went to town on her until she moaned her excitement, then turned it over to her sister. When they were both relieved, they were on their knees, taking turns sucking and stroking his cock. Just as he was about to blow, he heard shuffling against the rocky path.

"Uh, hey, Bron, brother, maybe you need to take that into your cottage," said Skull.

Avery had the decency to turn her back, his cock standing straight up, waiting to be serviced. His body weaved back and forth on the bench, and Skull gripped his arm, forcing him to stand. Skull helped him tuck his dick back in his pants, then turned to the women.

"Why are you two here?" he asked with a growl.

"Aren't they coushins?" he slurred.

"Not really," smirked Skull. "They're ex-wives of cousins, but they get invites that they should have the decency to decline. They're both looking for a way back into the family."

"Oh, shit," muttered Bron. Skull turned, grinning at Avery.

"I'll be there in about ten minutes, baby. Don't start without me. Let me get him back to his cottage."

"I'll take him," said Veda, smiling.

"No, you won't. I think you both need to leave. I'll let Mama Irene know what you did here tonight." Both women frowned, their faces noticeably paling even in the dim light of the gardens. They left quickly, and Avery kissed her husband.

"I'll be waiting," she purred.

Skull's dick jumped a mile, and he looked at the wobbling Bron and realized it was going to take him forever to get him to his cottage. Skull was a big bastard, six-feet-six and almost two-eighty, but Bron was no lightweight. Easily six-three, he probably weighed in at two-thirty. Keeping him upright was going to take forever, and Skull was not in the mood for patience tonight.

Instead, he tossed him over his shoulder and was outside his cottage in five minutes. He opened his door, poured him into bed, then left, locking him inside.

"Get some sleep, brother," he said to the closed door.

As sunlight filtered through the plantation shutters, Bron groaned, cursing Helios, the sun god. He rolled to his left too quickly, then realized he was about to do something he hadn't done in years.

Puke. Racing to the bathroom, he emptied the contents of his stomach, groaning the entire time. Finally able to stand, he turned on the shower and stepped beneath its steamy spray. He waited until he was clean, then switched it to ice cold water and screamed at himself.

On his third cup of coffee, it hit him. He nearly fucked an ex-wife of a Robicheaux cousin. Shit! He'd eaten both of them, and they were doing a damn fine job of sucking him off. He didn't want to show his face.

Fitch texted to ask if he wanted to go for a run. He declined. Doc texted to make sure he was feeling okay. He said, 'I'm fine.' Nothing could bring him out of his cottage. Nothing except a command from Cam Dougall.

"I don't understand why they're here to question me," said Bron. "I haven't been in my unit for almost two months now."

"We told them that," said Cam. "My Aunt Kari and Katarina are in the boardroom with CID now, waiting to question you. Just answer them honestly, Bron. We can vouch for where you were every minute of every day. Including last night." The Marine Corps Criminal Investigation Division, or CID, is a federal law enforcement agency run by the DOD. Something was definitely wrong.

"Fuck," he mumbled. "I'm sorry, Cam. Who do I owe apologies to?"

"No one, brother. Mama Irene asked me to find you. She saw that Veda and Elena were missing, and that usually means trouble. I don't know why she invites them to this shit, but they see a single man, and they're going in for the kill. Last night? You were easy pickins', brother. You okay?"

Bron nodded, following Cam down the hallway toward the boardroom.

"I'm so fucking sorry, Cam. I'm embarrassed as shit over that. I let the whole happily-ever-after bullshit, no offense, get to me."

"It's all good, Bron. You didn't do anything that any other single man wouldn't have done when it was offered up to him. Next time, just go home and get some sleep."

Now at the door of the boardroom, he couldn't fathom why he was being questioned in the death of a fellow MARSOC team member. What puzzled him was that he hadn't seen this man in years. In fact, they were never on the same team. They knew one another in passing and by name. But that was all.

"Bron, come on in," said Kari, waving to the chair between her and Katarina.

"Sgt. Bron Jones?" asked the CID agent. Bron nodded. "I'm Agent Mila Lambton. I'm the lead investigator in this case."

"I don't understand what this case is," he said, looking at the beautiful woman. She had dark brown hair tied in a severe bun at the nape of her neck. Her white oxford button-down was gaping at her bosom, but he could tell beneath that government bullshit she was pretty. Her light brown eyes had flecks of yellow, making her look like a cat.

"Sgt. Jones, do you know Sgt. Mike Hartfeld?" she asked.

"It's just Bron. I'm retired. And yes, I know Mike. He wasn't in my unit, but we knew of one another. We were both at Pendleton at the same time. Although it's huge, we're a tight-knit group, so I knew his name and his reputation."

"And did your ex-wife, Lora Jones, know Sgt. Hartfeld?" Bron frowned, looking at Kari, who gave him a nod.

"I don't know. We were only married for eight months, and six of those I was deployed. To my knowledge, Mike never came to the house, but they could have met on-base or at a function. Look, I really don't know anything about Lora's life. We've been divorced more than ten years. Once the ink was dry on our divorce papers, Lora pretty much disappeared from my life. I couldn't even find her to transfer her mail to her. She sent a few e-mails through my old military e-mail asking to speak with me, but I hadn't had a chance to call her back. Why aren't you asking her these questions?"

"Did she say what she wanted?" asked Agent Lambton, ignoring his question.

"No. She just said she really needed to speak with me, and she hoped I would call her or write back. She gave me a phone number and everything." He scanned through his phone and showed the message to the Agent, who only nodded. "Again, why aren't you asking her these questions?"

"I wish we could, Sgt. Jones. Five days ago, your ex-wife and Sgt. Hartfeld were seen leaving Pendleton with a rather large box in the back of his pickup truck. Apparently, in their infinite wisdom, the gate didn't look inside the box. We believe they were carrying classified files that we possessed on a potential secret Chinese weapons factory.

"They were followed up the coast and lost somewhere around Monterrey. Two days ago, we received a hit on our facial recognition. They checked into a place called Beresford Square, a hotel in San Francisco. When we arrived last night, your ex-wife was found dead alongside Sgt. Hartfeld's body. They were both naked and in an intimate embrace."

"Wh-what?" Bron thought he spoke, but he couldn't be sure. A tightness in his chest staggered him. The shock of Lora being dead took him by surprise. Actually, that wasn't it at all. The shock of knowing that she was with another Marine when she died hurt more. He wasn't even sure why. Out of his life for more than a decade, he didn't think about her much. They'd only had four months together before he was deployed, so that was hardly a basis for a relationship.

"I'm sorry, Sgt. Jones, but we believe that your ex-wife and Sgt. Hartfeld were spying for the Chinese, and someone caught them, literally, in the act. There were no weapons used, but there were high levels of a synthetic poison commonly used by the Chinese." Bron stood, staring at the people around the table.

"Bron? Where are you going, sweetie?" asked Katarina.

Bron turned to look at the room, frowning.

"I'm going to find a killer."

CHAPTER THREE

"Bron! Bron! Fucking stop now!" yelled Cam, Luke, and Eric following him. Eric stepped in front of him, staring down at his face. Bron didn't want to fight the big man, but he would if he had to.

"You're not going to stop me, Cam. We were only married a brief moment in time, but somebody killed her and a fellow Marine. I need to know the truth. A spy? That's not fucking Lora. No disrespect to my ex-wife, but she wasn't high on the IQ scale, and from what I can remember of Mike, neither was he. Now, I'm not saying that they couldn't have been in on something, but it seems unlikely to me."

"Bron, we understand, but you're not fucking doing this alone," said Luke. "You forget, you're part of a damn team now. We don't let brothers go off and do shit like this on their own."

Bron stared at the three men, nodding his head.

"Come back inside and speak to the CID. We'll figure this shit out. I promise you." Bron nodded, following the three men back inside. Stepping inside the boardroom, Kari gave him a sad smile and pointed to the chair once again.

"My apologies," he said, staring at the agent. "That was a shock, and all I could think of was finding who killed my ex-wife and brother Marine."

"That was quite a reaction for someone who's been divorced for more than ten years, Mr. Jones," said Agent Lambton.

"I told you, it's just Bron. I'm not sure how many cases you've investigated with the Marine Corps, Agent Lambton, but Marines don't just forget about people in their lives. I didn't love Lora any longer, maybe I never did, but I didn't wish harm to her. Besides, I can't believe that Lora or Mike had the ability to spy for the Chinese on a secret weapons factory."

"It's just Mila," she said, nervously shuffling the papers in front of her, not looking him in the eye. She pushed them back inside a folder, only to pull them back out again, straightening them once more. Bron stared at Luke, then Cam and Eric. All four men knew. Mila Lambton was lying.

"There is no weapons factory, is there, Agent Lambton?" asked Bron.

"What? Of course, there is, and I told you, it's just Mila."

"Mila, you have about fifty-nine seconds to tell me the fucking truth," said Luke. "If you don't, I'll be calling the CID myself to find out what your game is."

She leaned back in her seat, folding her arms across her chest defiantly. Luke grinned at her, mirroring her pose, as did the other men. Kat and Kari grinned, just watching the match of wills. Mila said nothing until Luke leaned forward.

"Thirteen, twelve, eleven," he said, reaching for his phone, "nine, eight, seven…" He hit the number for CID, and Mila Lambton practically shot out of her chair.

"Alright! Alright, I'll tell you why I'm here." Bron was furiously shaking his head at her. What sort of twisted, sick game was she playing?

"Is my ex-wife really dead?" he asked.

"Yes. I'm sorry. She is dead, and she was found in a bed with Mike Hartfeld in San Francisco. They also carried out a box of top-secret information from the base that was being held for a meeting that was supposed to take place next week. All of that was true."

"And are you really with CID?" asked Bron.

"I am. Lora was my roommate. She worked for UCSD in the admissions office. We both wanted to live in one of the trendier neighborhoods but couldn't afford it, so we decided to pool resources. I was gone a lot for work, and she worked full-time, so it worked well for us."

"Go on," said Bron.

"Lora was a good roommate. She stuck to herself, didn't interfere in my business, and never brought men back to the house. About four months ago, she and Mike Hartfeld started dating. I thought it was weird because she always said she'd never date another Marine as long as she lived. No offense."

"None taken," frowned Bron.

"Anyway, two weeks after they started dating, she tells me they're going on a vacation together to China. Again, I thought nothing of it. But then someone said that given the difficulties we're having with China right now, Mike wouldn't have been granted leave. So, I checked into it. He told his commanding officer that they were going to Alaska. They even bought tickets there.

"When she got back, I casually tried to ask her about the trip, but she said it didn't turn out as expected. After that, it felt as though she was trying to avoid me. I rarely saw her and didn't see Mike until about ten days ago. I got home from work, and he was sitting inside his car waiting for her. I stopped to talk to him and noticed the box in the backseat along with two large suitcases."

"Where did he say they were going?" asked Bron.

"He didn't, and when I asked Lora, she just brushed me off and said she'd be back soon. Something about it all felt wrong to me. I've never pried in Lora's business, but I just couldn't let it go. Every instinct in my body was telling me to investigate. So, I did. I carefully went through Lora's things and found these."

Taking several notebooks from her backpack and two historical books, she set them on the table, pushing them toward Bron, Luke, Cam, and Eric. They could see that they were copies, but they'd address that later.

"Genghis Kahn? I don't understand," said Bron.

"The photos and telemetry readings glued into this notebook are from a device called LIDAR. LIDAR, which stands for Light Detection and Ranging, is a remote sensing method that uses light in the form of a pulsed laser to measure ranges or variable distances to the Earth. It's a combination of 3-D scanning and laser scanning."

"Explain," said Cam, practically growling at the woman.

"The scanner, when pointed at any point on earth, sends hundreds of thousands of laser pulses which bounces back and gives a scanner reading that can tell you what's beneath a canopy of trees or a pile of dirt and grass. It's been used for a long time and in recent years, has helped to discover lost cities in Mexico, Peru, Egypt, Jordan, and other places. It's even helped in uncovering sunken ships.

"When the LIDAR scanned a hillside in Peru for possible signs of a lost city, the data was sent back to the labs, a computer programming model was able to remove the trees and other vegetation, and what was beneath was astonishing. A city, a lost city never before seen, hidden under hundreds, if not thousands of years of debris and growth."

"I'm still not following. Why would Lora have that kind of data for South America?" asked Bron.

"It wasn't for South America. It was of the lost tomb of Genghis Kahn." A man stopped in the doorway of the conference room, his large body practically filling the space. He pushed his wire-rimmed glasses up his nose and swallowed, staring at the table of people.

"Oh, hey, Thomas," said Cam. Thomas just stared at them. "Thomas? What's wrong?"

"Th-the lost tomb of Genghis Kahn has been a dream for every scientist or explorer for centuries. He once ruled everything between the Pacific Ocean and the Caspian Sea, but on his death, he asked to be buried in secret. His army was so distraught they carried his body home, killing anyone they met along the route. When they finally buried him, legend says that one thousand horses trampled over the gravesite to destroy any evidence of where he'd been buried."

"Why is any of that significant?" asked Bron.

"Because not only is it believed there is a vast treasure buried with him, but also a weapon of such great destruction, it would destroy the world if uncovered. Mongolians for years have been reluctant to allow anyone to search for it, the romanticizing making it a curse that is said to destroy the world if uncovered.

"Part of that comes from the legend of Tamarlane, a 14th-Century Turkic-Mongolian king whose tomb was opened in 1941 by Soviet archaeologists. Immediately after that tomb was disturbed, Nazi soldiers invaded the Soviet Union. Many thought it was a by-product of opening the tomb.

"Folklore holds that Genghis Khan was buried on a peak in the Khentii Mountains, but historians have never been able to actually locate the spot at the peak called Burkhan Khaldun. They also say that if the tomb is found and opened, the world will end as we know it today."

"Wow, you really know a lot about this," said Mila.

"I know a lot about a lot of things," said Thomas plainly. Luke stared at Thomas, grinning. "Oh, right. I know a lot about this because of the legend of the weapon. Scientists have speculated as to whether it's a biological weapon or some rare mineral that Kahn discovered, but no one has ever been able to find it."

"Well, I think Lora and Mike found it," said Mila. "All of this information led them back to China and Mongolia. In that hotel room in San Francisco, they found two plane tickets to Beijing. They also found the name of a well-known guide who was scheduled to take them on a four-day tour of the wall. No offense to anyone, but typical tours of the wall are a day long, not four days.

"I think they were going to head to a remote part of the wall, go over the side to Mongolia, and move on to find this location. My only question is, why? Were they looking for the weapon?"

Bron stood from his seat, circling the table slowly, his hand rubbing the back of his neck. Mila noticed the muscles flexing through his t-shirt and swallowed. He was big, like the other men in the room, but there was something exotically sexy about him. His latte skin and wavy dark hair made her think he was Hispanic at first, but there was something about his bone structure that said he might be Caribbean or African. Either way, he was hot as hell.

"Let me get this straight. You think my ex-wife and Mike Hartfeld were headed to Mongolia to find the lost tomb of Genghis Kahn and a potential unknown weapon. And do what?"

"I don't know," said Mila. "Honestly, I have no idea. But the problem is, whoever killed them does have an idea. That individual knows everything that we know, maybe more. What I have are preliminary maps and findings in the area, but what if they had more in that hotel room? The killer may have a jump on us to get to the location."

Bron stared at the woman, her eyes pleading for help. Her smooth skin was a beautiful hue of gold like she enjoyed laying by a pool or on a beach. He pictured that body in a bikini and felt his cock jump just slightly, then shook his head.

"We're not treasure hunters. That's not what we do," he said. "I'm sorry, but I can't help you." He started toward the door, and Mila jumped to her feet.

"Wait! Please. I can't do this without help. I know you have no feelings for Lora, and I don't blame you. She told me what she did to you, but I do think she and Mike were happy together. Lora was my roommate and my friend, and I don't have a lot of friends. She didn't deserve to be poisoned lying in bed with someone she loved."

Bron felt an anger rise in his chest, then just as suddenly, it disappeared. He didn't love Lora any longer, and he seriously doubted if he ever did. It was ego. His ego was hurt because she chose to have a long-term relationship with another Marine.

"What are you proposing?" asked Cam.

"I'm simply asking for a little help with this. I contacted the guide that they originally scheduled, and he's available next week. I'm going, with or without help, but I'd really like someone there with me."

"Why? Why would you care?" asked Bron. "She's gone. Nothing you do will bring her back. Going to China right now with the political climate the way it is, is insanity. If you're caught going over the wall into Mongolia, you'll be arrested. Why not just apply for the visa and fly into Mongolia?"

"It takes too long. That's why they were going through Beijing. The guide will pick us up from the hotel and drive us to the most northern point, where we'll stay at a hotel near the wall. I've asked him to leave us from there. I need to find out what's there, Bron. If I don't, we may end up with world war three."

"She's right," said Thomas, staring at his friends. "Kahn was ruthless, but he was also ingenious. He used weapons that others had never seen before. He was one of the first to use strategic warfare, guerilla fighting, and more. It's quite possible that he found a weapon, man-made, earth-made, or chemical, that he didn't get the chance to unleash on the world."

"Are you seriously proposing that we go with her?" asked Bron.

"I'm saying we should consider it."

"Where are you staying?" asked Eric.

"I haven't checked into my hotel yet, but I have a room at the Fairmont." She shifted from one foot to the other, looking down at the table.

"No, that's too far from here," said Eric. "We've got cottages available. You can stay here until we can figure out what the hell is going on. Give us a day or so to contact some people we know in the government to see if they've heard any rumblings of what's happening. We'll try to give you an answer soon."

"Are you sure? I mean, it's no trouble for me to go back into town and stay," she said, looking at the room of people. Cam and Luke looked toward Bron. Frowning, he stood and nodded.

"Follow me," he said. "We'll ask Mama Irene which of the cottages she wants to give you."

"I don't know what any of that means but thank you. Look, I don't know what you all will decide, but I have to figure this out. I want to know what happened to Lora, but I also want to stop whatever this maniac is trying to do. If he was willing to kill two people, it can't be good."

"Just give us some time," said Luke. She nodded, following Bron from the room. When she was gone, Luke, Cam, and Eric looked at Thomas. Kari and Kat were still seated on the other side of the table.

"Thomas? Why should we do this?" asked Eric.

"Beyond the significance of the archaeological find? I mean, just finding Kahn's tomb would be historic, in and of itself. But finding this alleged weapon, that's another matter. It's been speculated that it could be anything from a biological weapon to an unknown element that could have a nuclear type of effect.

"Finding the tomb is a dream for anyone, especially an archaeologist, which I am not. However, I would still love to prove its existence and forever put to rest any thoughts on what this weapon is."

"So," grinned Luke, "that's a yes?"

"Oh, yea," laughed Thomas. "That's a yes from me. In fact, I'd like to be part of the team that goes with Mila and Bron, but I would also suggest that we bring an archaeologist. Maybe Adele knows of someone at the university."

"Okay, let's find out what we're hearing on the internet, through any other channels, and meet again in the morning. Thomas? Make a list of anything you might need for the expedition and contact Adele. We can either send it with you or buy it when you get there."

"Cool," he smiled. "Very cool."

CHAPTER FOUR

Mila grabbed her bag from the backseat of her rental car and followed the brooding man in front of her. His ass was rock-solid and filled out the blue jeans he was wearing better than anyone she'd ever known, man or woman. His narrow waist, nipped above the strong buttocks, led to a wide, muscular back. His wavy black hair made her want to run her fingers through it.

Losing herself in his physique, he stopped suddenly, and she wasn't paying attention. Slamming into his back, she bounced backwards and fell on her ass against the path.

"Ouch," she mumbled.

"Are you okay?" he asked, kneeling beside her. He ran his hands up and down her arms, then up and down her legs.

"I'm okay, nothing broken except my pride," she frowned. "Sorry, I was lost in thought." He nodded, helping her to her feet and then up the steps to the cottage. Bron opened the door and set her bags down.

"We're not very formal here," he said, staring at her black pantsuit. "You might want to change into something more comfortable for lunch. We do almost all of our meals in the big cafeteria by the offices. Whenever you're ready, come on over."

"I'd love it if you would wait for me. I mean, if you'll give me five minutes, I'll change," she said. "I'd love to ask you some questions." He nodded, frowning at her as she took her bag to the bedroom. He noticed she didn't close the bedroom door and then knew why.

"I wanted to tell you that Lora regretted leaving you like she did," called Mila from the bedroom. "She knew it was a young, stupid mistake and really regretted not being more mature about it."

Bron said nothing, staring down at his feet. He didn't want to talk about this. He'd made peace with it a decade ago and didn't need to rehash it now.

"If it matters at all to you, she didn't date much. She always said she wouldn't date another Marine, which is why I was surprised when she and Mike started dating."

"It doesn't matter, but I thought Mike was married," called Bron down the hallway.

"He was. His wife left him about three years ago, ironically, for a guy in the Coast Guard."

Bron grinned to himself. That must have hurt. Mila came down the hallway toward him, and he swallowed, trying not to react to her. She wore a pair of white jeans, the hems frayed at the bottom. On her feet, she wore a pair of gold sandals that matched the gold of her top. With her hair hanging around her shoulders, he noticed that it wasn't as dark as he'd originally thought. Waves of brown, red, gold, and auburn wove through the tresses, the golden highlight of her eyes blinking at him.

"I'm ready," she said.

"Wh-what?"

"I said, I'm ready. Unless this isn't okay. You said casual," she smiled.

"Yea, I mean, no, you're fine. I mean, what you're wearing is okay. It gets kind of loud and crazy in the cafeteria, so just expect a lot of noise."

"Oh, it's no problem at all," she smiled.

"How long were you a Marine?" he asked.

"Well, technically, I still am. Just because I'm CID doesn't mean I'm not still a Marine," she smiled. "I'll have fifteen years in about three months. I haven't really decided if I will leave then or not, but I know that it's getting harder to do my job. Political bullshit, red tape, all that lovely stuff. I got my degree in criminal justice while I was doing my first four years and then started working toward CID."

"How did you and Lora meet?" asked Bron.

"I used to run the trails around the zoo path in San Diego, and one day I came upon her and her bike. She had a flat and didn't have a patch kit with her. I helped her carry the bike back to her car, and she offered to buy me coffee. We started talking about how expensive it was to live in San Diego, and the idea of rooming together came to us."

Bron frowned, nodding his head. Lora had never exercised a day in her life. It didn't mean she hadn't taken it up, but why cycling, and why now? It all seemed far too convenient.

"So, you roomed together? Just like that?"

"No, not just like that. She was in a lease for another three months, and I had two months left on mine. We agreed we would spend some time together and see how we got along. It was great."

"And are you based at Pendleton?" asked Bron.

"I know what you're trying to ask, Bron. She didn't know me before we met. There would have been no reason for our paths to cross, and why would she have needed me if she had Mike on-base already. Believe me, I've run everything through my head a million times. It's what I do for a living."

"I'm sorry, I didn't mean to offend you. It just seems very strange that Lora would suddenly start cycling while you were running, choose to get a roommate, and then choose to date another Marine stationed at Pendleton where this information is being held. That's a lot of coincidences."

She said nothing as they walked the path toward the large glass structure. For the first time since she'd arrived, Mila looked up and around the property.

"Wow, this is really beautiful. The cottages are so lovely, and that mansion is amazing. It's like I've stepped back in time," she said, turning in a circle. Bron watched as she spun around, her hair flowing in a circle around her shoulders.

"Yea," he squeaked out, then cleared his throat. "Yea, the whole property belongs to the Robicheaux family. It's really something."

Inside the cafeteria, people were rushing back and forth, gathering their midday meal and chatting with family and friends around them. He placed a hand on her back and pointed to a group of tables where Thomas, Cam, Luke, Ajei, Sophia Ann, and Adele were talking. Clay stood behind his wife, a protective arm around her shoulders.

While Mila filled her plate, chatting casually with George, Bron stared at his friends.

"Adele has someone who is willing to go with you. She's a young professor specializing in archaeology in Asia and Africa. We haven't given her any information, just that she would be accompanying our team to China to potentially search for a historical artifact," said Cam.

"Do you think she'll still go when she finds out what we're looking for?" asked Bron.

"Oh, hell yes," smiled Adele. "I want to go, but my big angry bear won't let me."

"I'm not a big angry bear, but you're not going to fucking China when the whole country is a powder keg."

"I know, baby," she smiled. "Let me know if you want her to come here to meet with us. She's available."

"Arrange for her to come out tonight for dinner, Aunt Adele," said Luke. "We'll get her take on what we know and what Mila found. Let me check with the tech team to see what was found at the murder site in San Francisco."

"Hello," said Mila, standing at the table with a tray of food. They all looked at the piles of deliciousness and grinned. "I don't eat this much, but that man over there said I had to try everything. I didn't want to offend him." Bron grinned.

"You won't offend him. Eat what you want, but you don't have to eat it all," he said.

"Oh, good," she said, taking a seat. "I was worried. I mean, it all smells amazing and looks amazing, but this is a lot! Although, I did notice that woman over there with two trays as big as mine." She nodded toward Britt, and they all smiled.

"Hi, I'm Adele Robicheaux Duffy," said Adele with an extended hand. "My parents own this property, and my brothers were all original members of RP. I happen to be a professor of history at Tulane University."

"Oh, wow! I've come to the right place. Do you know anything about Kahn and his lost tomb?" she asked.

"Well, everything I know, you could probably get off the internet or in a book, but I know that Kahn literally means emperor. He was the first emperor of the Mongol Empire. He was born Temüjin but was later called Genghis Kahn. He actually lived a pretty long life for someone of that time period, and considering his lifestyle.

"He launched his campaign for power all across Asia and then ultimately all the way to Europe, as far north as Poland and south to Egypt. Some saw him as a ruthless conqueror. Others saw him as a liberator. He was ahead of his time in many ways. He practiced meritocracy, encouraged religious tolerance, and by all accounts, he brought the Silk Road under one political environment.

"He died in 1227 while fighting at Yinchuan, or at least that's one story. Some historians say he fell from his horse while hunting. Others say he died from infection due to an arrow wound. No one really knows. Whether we see him as a hero or villain, even today, his name and likeness appear on coins, buildings, street signs, even liquor and candy. What you say that your friend found has been a mystery for almost eight hundred years. If it's real, and if she knew where to find it, I can only imagine what others might do to get to it," said Adele.

"That's kind of what I'm worried about," muttered Mila. Adele smiled, nodding at the young woman but staring at her beautiful face.

"If you don't mind me saying so, Mila, your features are quite striking. You must have an interesting heritage," smiled Adele.

"Oh, well, thank you. I'm a mix, I suppose. According to DNA tests, I'm Greek and Spanish, Irish and German. I've noticed that none of you were short-changed in the genetic line-up. If I had to guess, there are about fifty of you directly related, and I'm fairly certain that the woman sitting over there is your twin."

"That's right," laughed Adele. "Chances are pretty good that if they have auburn hair and whiskey-colored eyes, they're related. We're all Robicheauxs."

"That must be so wonderful," she said quietly, her eyes filling with tears. Bron frowned at Adele, who reached out to touch the woman's arms. "Sorry, I didn't mean to react that way. It's just that I didn't know my parents. I was left at the hospital after I was born. According to the nurses, my father brought my mother in, supported her while she was in labor, and they both cried happily when I was born. A few hours later, she heard me crying in the crib and came in to find them both gone."

"I'm so sorry," said Adele.

"It's okay. I was in an orphanage for a number of years and then was adopted when I was six. It wasn't the best of lives for me, but I had a roof over my head and food."

Bron stared at her, wanting to ask all the questions that were running through his head, but he held back. They chatted casually after that until lunch was done, and then Bron took her back to her cottage.

"I'll come back for you when it's time for dinner," he said, keeping his distance from her. Nodding, she gave him a weak smile and shut the cottage door, leaning her back against it. Pulling out the copies of Lora's notebooks once again, she flipped through the pages, finding the last entry.

The tomb can be found at the base of the furthest cliff, where the world will find its end.

CHAPTER FIVE

"What are your thoughts on all this, Bron?" asked Cam, shoving his hand through his dark hair as the others in the room grinned, the action looking identical to his father's.

"I did some reading on Kahn and the legend of the tomb. Everything Adele said was right. He was a warrior. Some considered him evil. Others considered him good. His sons and grandsons took over for years after he died. The thing that's common in all the materials I read were his instructions to keep his burial site a secret.

"However, one thing I found, written by a Chinese scholar in the seventeenth century, was a bit different. It said that toward the end of his life, he regretted the conquering and war, and although he possessed the ability to rule all the nations, he didn't follow through on it. What if this mysterious weapon he found was in his hands the whole time, but he saw the wisdom in not using it? He actually had it buried with him."

"Brother, I hope that's true," said Cam. "Whatever this weapon is, we need to find it first. The treasure I could give a shit about, but I'm happy to turn it over to Adele and her colleague."

"Cam, if we find it, we have to turn it over to the Mongols," said Adele. "You need to be prepared to claim that you were simply hiking in the area and got lost. If they think you're there to do anything except sight-seeing, you'll be thrown in jail unless you have a permit to explore."

"Fuck," he muttered.

"The Chinese are extremely suspicious and cautious of Americans, Bron," said Adele. "May Wong, the archaeologist who is coming, is a Chinese American. She speaks both simple and Mandarin Chinese, and she'll act as a bridge for you."

"Actually," said the tiny woman stepping inside the room, "it would be best if you let me do all of the talking. Hello, I'm May Wong."

"May, it's so great to see you again," said Adele, hugging the other woman. "Thank you for coming out."

"You mention Kahn's tomb to me, and I'd be an idiot not to come out here," she laughed. She looked at Bron and nodded. "I'm sorry about your ex-wife."

"Thank you." There wasn't anything else to say. He truly didn't have any feelings about her death one way or another.

"Hello," she said, looking at Thomas.

"Hello," he said, staring at the woman. She was maybe five-feet-four, her porcelain skin had a soft blush to it, the almond-shaped brown eyes had thick black lashes fluttering around them. Jet-black hair fell to her shoulders in a straight, sharp bob, swinging with every movement she made.

"Um, you are?" she grinned.

"Oh, sorry," said Thomas, blushing. "I'm Dr. Thomas Bradshaw. I'll be going with you on this trip."

"Dr. Bradshaw," she repeated. "Aren't you a PhD in physics, astrophysics, and geology?" Thomas smiled at the woman.

"Yes, but how does an archaeologist know that?"

"You were the person who perfected a way to test sediment for chemical compounds found in meteors and volcanoes, allowing us the opportunity to date historic sites in less time." Thomas nodded as the room grinned, witnessing a potential budding relationship.

"When you're done," smirked Cam.

"Oh, sorry, of course. I was just thinking if it's just going to be myself, Dr. Bradshaw, the military woman, and you," she said, pointing to Bron, "it might be best if we portrayed ourselves as married couples. That way, there wouldn't be any suspicion or judgment of us traveling together."

"I'm fine with that," said Bron. "It will also ensure that there is a layer of protection for you and Mila at night. We can figure out the appropriate sleeping arrangements. Do you have family or friends in China? Someone we could call on if we need assistance?"

"I actually have an aunt and uncle who live in Mongolia. I have not told them I'm coming as I wanted to be sure that you all needed me first and, second, I don't want to use traditional phone lines. My uncle was an archaeologist as well, and he's fairly certain they're bugging his phone lines."

"We will definitely need you," said Thomas quickly. She raised a brow with a grin and nodded.

"I'll let them know I'm planning a visit with friends to hike the mountains. They can make sure the officials in the area know, and everything will be seen as a legal, friendly excursion. I'd also advise that we get to Beijing sooner rather than later. We need to look like tourists, and when I tell you the Chinese are suspicious enough to watch our every move, they will watch our every move."

"Alright, but what about this tomb and the potential hidden weapon?" asked Bron. "We're happy to give you credit for the archaeological find, but we need to make sure that weapon doesn't get in the wrong hands."

"I agree," said May. "Like any other industry in this world, archaeology has its dark side as well. There are groups of bandit archaeologists who are untrained and don't really care about the damage they do to a site of historical importance.

"In years past, we saw it happen all too often with tombs in Egypt, Turkey, and Syria. Before the governments took hold, Greece and Rome were being pillaged for their ruins. Thank goodness someone realized the significance of places like Athens, Rome, Pompeii, and so many more. They all would have been destroyed if not for an awakening of their importance. I don't think Kahn knew that his tomb would be sought after, but I do think he knew that others would attempt to find what he had, meaning both the treasure and the weapon."

"Dr. Wong, do you have any idea what this weapon could be?" asked Thomas.

"It's just May," she smiled. "No. Gunpowder had already been invented and, in fact, Kahn was using it in war. Not in guns but in other ways. I honestly don't know. What we do know is that there are a number of prehistoric sites in northern China and Mongolia, along the Russian border, that we believe were struck by meteors thousands of years ago. That leaves us wide open to whatever space has to offer or he could have found it during one of his conquests in another part of the world."

"Damn," muttered Luke.

"May, is it possible that there is no weapon at all?" asked Thomas.

"Dr. Bradshaw, Thomas, may I call you Thomas?" she asked sweetly. He nodded, smiling at her. "Anything is possible. This isn't a tomb that was found and then lost. It's been lost since the beginning. It also could be a bunch of bullshit. Kahn or his men might have perpetuated this myth in order to keep people away from his tomb."

"We need to find that tomb and then get the hell out of there," said Luke. "Thomas has the LIDAR scanner, and he's made some modifications."

"You have LIDAR?" said May, somewhat surprised.

"We do," grinned Thomas. "I made some changes to it, but it can now help me to differentiate between man-made objects and those that are natural to the surrounding area. I can input the exact location we are standing at, and the readings will decipher if something is natural or unnatural to the area. It will also penetrate through certain types of rock, whereas before, it would not."

"That's amazing," she whispered, staring up at him. "I'd love to learn more."

"Of course," said Thomas, crooking his elbow. "If you'd like, I can escort you to dinner, and we can talk about it over George's famous brisket." May smiled, sliding her slender hand into his arm.

"I have no idea who George is, but I love brisket. Much to my mother's dismay, I'm not a fan of Chinese food. I'm an American woman who likes beef, French fries, and chocolate chip cookies." They heard them chatting as they moved down the hallway toward the door, and Eric and Luke could only laugh, shaking their heads.

"Well," smiled Adele. "It looks as though we might get a two for one deal with May."

"Did you know that would happen?" asked Luke with a sly grin. "Aunt Adele, are you taking over for Grandma?"

"Moi?" she said with an exaggerated expression of surprise. She laughed, leaving them inside the boardroom and heading to the grove where they would enjoy another beautiful evening outside.

"Bron? Are you sure you want to follow this through?" asked Luke.

"I have to. Someone has to, and since I was the one married to Lora, it does seem I'm the likely choice. Besides, if this weapon is something beyond what we already know, I might be the best person, along with Thomas, to identify it. If it's highly unstable, we might need to find a way to neutralize it or, I hate to say this, detonate whatever it is."

"Okay, I think we need to send a few guys along to be tourists in Beijing for a few days. Just in case. That way, you'll have help if you need it, but nothing too close that would alarm anyone." Bron nodded as they all stood to head to dinner.

"The more, the merrier."

CHAPTER SIX

Mila read and reread the copies of the documents that Lora had left in her bedroom. She'd given the originals to the team but felt the need to keep copies for herself. When she found them neatly stacked beneath Lora's bed, she just knew they weren't private journals. Lora wasn't the type to write in a private journal.

Staring at them, it wasn't the first time she wondered if perhaps the notebooks were fakes, or perhaps they were the real ones, the ones in the hotel room being fake. Anything was possible, and she could picture Mike thinking in a covert, spy way. Perhaps he was the one that encouraged her to do this. She knew that Mike was struggling with alimony and child support payments.

In fact, Lora had confided in Mila that she'd lent him money to get caught up so he wouldn't get into trouble with the Marine Corps.

She looked at the map once again, identifying the area suspected of holding Kahn's tomb, and shook her head. This wouldn't be an easy climb or find, even if they could find it. Her only hope was Bron and the RP team, who had the technology that could help her in the excavation. But it was really the murder of her friend and roommate that she wanted solved.

When she'd been notified that Lora was murdered while on vacation, she was devastated. They'd been good friends and even better roommates. It didn't take long, and she was tying her find in Lora's room to the deaths. CID refused to assign the case to her given the close nature of her relationship with Lora, but she requested every ounce of leave she had. Seventeen days and she was already down two.

If she weren't back at Pendleton in fifteen days, she would be considered AWOL. If they planned it properly, they could get to Mongolia, locate the tomb site, and hopefully be back within the week. Looking at all the papers on the table, she shoved them aside and leaned back in the chair.

"Who are you kidding?" she mumbled to herself. "This won't be solved in a few days. No one has even attempted to find this in decades." The knock on the front door made her jump, and her first instinct was to reach for her service weapon, which was suddenly no longer where she'd left it. Opening the door, she smiled up at Bron, then looked back at the table.

"Looking for this?" he said, holding up her weapon.

"Hey! You had no right to take that," she huffed, reaching for the weapon in his hand.

"We had every right to take that," he said, stepping inside the cottage. "You're on RP property, and you didn't tell us you were carrying weapons. We checked the serial number on this and verified that it was CID issued. Now, you can have it back."

"All you had to do was ask me," she frowned.

"You were asked by Code when he let you in the gates if you had any weapons. You told him 'no.'"

Mila could feel her face flushing a bright red and turned back to the table, gathering her documents and shoving them back in the accordion file. Bron watched every move she made, still unsure of whether or not he could trust the woman.

"I'm sorry, you're right. I wasn't sure how you would feel about Lora, and honestly, when you stormed out of the room, I just thought you were still in love with her."

"And you suspected if I were still in love with her that maybe I killed them?" he said with a fierce expression.

"No! I mean, maybe. I knew that you most likely didn't know about Kahn's tomb, but I'm honestly just trying to find out who killed them. The rest is important, but not as important as me finding out who poisoned them. Your reaction seemed odd for a man that only dated the woman two months and technically was only married and together two months before you were deployed."

"First, if you talk to any of the couples here, you'd find out that being married within two months of meeting is normal. And second, you could just leave it to CID," said Bron, leaning against the doorjamb, his arms folded over his chest. She swallowed, seeing the flex of his forearms and that gorgeous skin color.

"I could. So could you. I need to know why finding this was so important to Lora and Mike. Neither were archaeologists and had no interest in it, from what I know. So why? Why were they trying to find Kahn's tomb, and was it because of this weapon?" She reached for the door, and Bron gripped her wrist, his huge hand encircling her tiny bones. She tried to pull back, which only served to force her forward, against his body.

"I'm doing this because you brought it to my doorstep," said Bron in a low, rumbling bass. His face was mere inches from her own, the big golden eyes staring up at him. "You could have just called and told me she'd died, and I wouldn't have cared either way. Instead, you came here and told me she'd been murdered. You brought this to my door. Why?" She tried to pull her hand free, but to no avail, squirming.

"Let me go," she ground out between her clenched teeth.

"Tell me why," he smiled. He could smell her perfume and grinned down at her. That damn gold top was askew, her lush, round breasts peeking from the neckline.

"I needed help! Okay? There, that's why I came to you. I needed help. I can't do this alone." She said in frustration. "Lora told me that you were MARSOC, and I heard from someone on-base that you'd retired and gone to work for RP. There. Are you happy now?" Bron thread his hands through her hair.

"Not yet," he growled, crashing his mouth against her own, prying her lips open with his tongue. She tried to push back, then fell into him, her hands fisting his t-shirt as he spun her around, slamming her body against the wall. Bending his knees slightly, he ground his stiff cock into her, and she gasped at the sensations coursing through her body.

When her hands touched the hot flesh of his back, he let a rumble escape his gut, up through his throat, and then pulled back. She looked dazed and uncertain of her surroundings, blinking up at him. Bron was breathless, staring at her.

"I'm sorry," he said, shaking his head. "I shouldn't have done that. Come on, let's get to the grove for dinner."

Mila was speechless. He was sorry. What was he sorry for? Rocking her world with just one kiss or lighting a fire in her body that could never be extinguished. Which was it?

"Y-you go ahead," she whispered. "I need a few minutes."

"Mila..."

"Please, Bron. Just give me a few minutes. I'll be there shortly." He nodded, leaving her cottage, but it didn't escape him that her eyes were filled with tears, and he was the dickhead that put them there.

He stepped off the porch, started toward the grove, then stopped, looking back at the cottage. Shaking his head, he turned around, taking a seat on the steps. He would wait for her. Wait and apologize.

CHAPTER SEVEN

"Holy hell in a handbasket," she muttered, touching her lips.

She'd been kissed in her lifetime, a lot, but never had a man kissed her so fiercely with such intensity and yearning that she was left confused. Every part of her body was on fire, aching for one more touch of the man. This was stupid. Stupid, stupid, stupid! How was she going to make it with him next to her for the next week?

"I need to leave," she whispered. Then shaking her head, she knew that wasn't an option unless she wanted to leave it all to chance. No. She had to solve Lora and Mike's murder and at least try to find this secret weapon.

She splashed cold water on her face, patting it dry, then collected herself and headed back out the door of the cottage. Mila was surprised to see Bron sitting on the steps. He stood, and she just stared back at him.

"Mila, I'm sorry. That was out of line. I had no right to do that, and I apologize."

"What are you apologizing for? I mean, are you sorry you kissed me or sorry that I kissed you back?" she asked with hurt in her eyes.

"Honestly? I'm not sure, Mila. Listen, for some reason, I haven't exactly been making the right choices lately. The only good thing I did was retire from the Marines and come here to RP. I don't want to do anything to fuck that up. I was just standing so close to you, and you were staring at me with those golden eyes…"

"Amber. They're amber."

"Right, amber," he mumbled, thinking that didn't make it any damn better. "I was staring at you, and then your perfume hit me, and, well, I just lost it, okay?"

"Okay," she said, taking a step toward him.

"Okay?"

"Yea, no big deal. I mean, we're adults. Friends kiss all the time. We can be friends, right?" He gave a short nod, and she grinned. "Good. We're friends."

Standing on the same step where Bron was perched, she leaned forward and kissed him. Nothing quite as earth-shattering as his kiss, but it was enough to slide her tongue along his lips and hear him moan. She quickly turned and began walking toward the grove.

"Come on," she called back, "we don't want to be late for dinner."

It took Bron about thirty seconds to calm his breathing and straighten his dick, but he followed her to the grove, then got his food, and sat at the opposite end of the table. She sat next to Thomas and May. At their table were also Luke, Adele, Ajei, Doc, Cam, Eric, and Sophia Ann. Sophia Ann pushed several items toward Mila.

"Mila and May, the bracelet and necklace are both trackers and emergency responders. If you're taken, we can find you via the satellite links in the jewelry, but there are also buttons on the backs of the stones that, when depressed, send distress signals to us. These international cell phones will have the ability to track you as well. They are capable of audio-recording, video, and allow you to conduct a number of readings. Everything from soil sampling, temperature, altimeter, and much more."

"This is unbelievable," said Mila, putting the jewelry on. She struggled with the necklace, and someone behind her helped hook the clasp.

"There you go, beautiful," said Fitch, grinning at the woman.

"Oh, hello. Thank you. I'm Mila."

"Fitch. Patrick Fitch, but just call me Fitch," he smiled. They heard a strange rumbling, and Sophia Ann looked to see if one of the dogs was beneath the table, but it was Fitch that stared at his friend and laughed, shaking his head.

"Mila, this is May Wong. She is the archaeologist that works with Adele. She'll be going with you to China and Mongolia, as well as Thomas. The four of you will need to pretend to be couples enjoying a travel experience together."

"Couples?" swallowed Mila.

"Yes," said May. "I recommended that as it will allow us to stay closer together. I've also recommended that a team go with us, just to pretend to be tourists, but available if we need help." Luke nodded, then spoke again.

"We're sending Fitch, Hiro, and..."

"Me," smiled the huge man walking toward them. He was easily six-feet-six, two hundred and ninety pounds of rock-hard muscle. His brown hair and green eyes lent a boyish charm to an otherwise manly face, the stubble making all the girls look twice.

"Fucking asshole," grinned Cam. "CC? What the hell are you doing home?"

"Brother, I am officially retired. Hello," said CC, staring at the others. "I'm CC, Charles Corbett Neill. My father is Max, and my mother is that beautiful doctor over there, Riley."

"Hello," smiled Mila.

"Hi," blushed May. Thomas and Bron both frowned at the other man, nodding.

"Luke thought it might be a good idea for me to get my feet wet on this one," grinned CC. "Besides, I know Hiro Tanaka really well. We served together in a few fine, government-assigned locations. Between me, Hiro, and Fitch, we'll be good." Fitch reached for the big man's hand and shook it, almost wincing at the fierce grip.

"Nice to meet you, brother," said Fitch. "Heard a lot about you."

"Same, man. Savannah is taking the three of us to Beijing tonight. We're going in for a guys' getaway, couple of rich cats on Daddy's jet."

"Nice," smirked Bron.

"Oh, don't worry, big man," laughed CC. "You all will be flying first-class to Beijing. We're staying at the same hotel as you, and we'll leave you an itinerary of the places you need to visit and when to arrive. I'm grabbing my gear, and we'll see you there. Ladies? Watch out for these two." He winked at the women and left.

"Damn, who was that?" asked May. Thomas frowned at her again.

"CC is the only son of Max and Riley, as he said," said Cam. "He's been in the Army almost twenty years now. I know they're glad he's home, and so are we. He's a big bastard with his father's God-given natural strength, and thankfully, his mother's fine brain. He also has a degree in chemistry, so we thought he might be a good addition."

"That makes sense," said May. "Well, listen, after we spoke, I reached out casually to a few peers, just asking if there were any interesting digs happening. No one said a word about anything happening in that region. There are some things happening in Central America and the Sudan, but nowhere else."

"The Sudan?" questioned Bron. "What could they be doing there? That place is a fucking mess."

"It is, but it has more pyramids and ancient tombs than Egypt, and archaeologists have been struggling to save them for decades now. A few are now underwater due to the changes in the Nile. There have been some incredible finds." Thomas was staring at May like most women stare at chocolate. Bron smirked to himself, wondering if this was Thomas's first crush.

"So, what now?" asked Mila.

"Get some sleep, pack for the trip, and we'll take you to the airport in the morning," said Cam. "You have a flight to San Francisco with a three-hour layover, then you'll be going on to Beijing. Remember, act like couples. If you can't do that, tell me now, and we'll have to find another cover."

"I'm good," said Thomas.

"Same," said Bron, staring at Mila.

"I'm fine with it," said May. She looked toward Mila, her face flush with excitement or embarrassment, perhaps both.

"I'm fine," she said in barely a whisper. Cam looked at Bron, wondering if something had happened between the two, then just shrugged.

"Alright. May? We're counting on you to get us there. Thomas and Bron, make sure nothing happens to these two. We're going to use the stealth netting to cover the weapons, but you better be damn sure where you're carrying them and who you pull them on. A Chinese prison is not something I want to have to break into."

Both men nodded, Bron jerked his head toward Thomas as they stepped outside the atrium of the grove.

"I know you can handle a weapon, Thomas, but are you prepared to kill someone if we need to?" asked Bron.

"I'm prepared," he said. "You may not know this, Bron, but I was a child when I helped Ian's team kill my Russian grandfather with my technology. I know you already know this, but I'm different. Yes, I'm smart, but unlike many very smart people, I have a keen sense of emotional self-awareness and can usually disassociate from any situation in order to complete a project or mission."

"I'm not doubting you, Thomas. I'm sorry if it sounded that way. I just want to be sure we can protect Mila and May." Thomas nodded, looking back over his shoulder at the petite woman. "She's beautiful, isn't she?"

"Yes. She's the prettiest woman I've ever met, and she's smart," said Thomas.

"Tell her that," grinned Bron. Thomas turned to the man chuckling.

"Bron, I'm not a virgin. I've dated women before. Many. You'd be surprised how much ass you can get as the genius professor or researcher. I suppose I took advantage of that in my early twenties, a lot like you guys took advantage of your uniform for it. I just don't want to start something that I might not be able to finish or that might distract me while we're there."

"Sorry, brother. I wasn't implying you were a virgin, but it's good to know you used your assets to help yourself," laughed Bron.

"I'm not proud of that," said Thomas, shaking his head. "My brain might have been advanced, but my dick certainly wasn't. It had the same base, caveman instincts as every other man on the planet. I'm just glad I was smart enough to use condoms."

"Amen to that, brother."

"Do you like Mila?" he asked.

"She's damn sure beautiful," said Bron. "I'm just not so sure she's told us everything we need to know. I'm trying to trust her, but there's something holding me back."

"Maybe it's because she knew your ex-wife. Don't associate the two," said Thomas. "Mila is nothing like Lora from what you've said. For what it's worth, Bron, I don't think she's lying to us. I'm pretty good at seeing those fluctuations in people's faces, and I don't see that with her." Bron nodded.

"Well, I guess I need to get my shit packed. If we're going into the mountains, I need cold-weather climbing gear. Let's finish dinner, and we can make sure everyone has what they need."

"Bron? Thanks for letting me come along on this one," he grinned.

"I'm damn glad you are, Thomas. I'm gonna need that big brain of yours and probably those big muscles, too. You been working out with Tailor?" he laughed. Thomas laughed, shaking his head.

"No. God help me, but I've been working out with Rory, Trak, and Hiro."

CHAPTER EIGHT

It was nearly eleven p.m. when Mila heard the soft knock on her door. She knew the property was secure, so she wasn't concerned about an intruder, but she didn't know who it might be. Opening the door, she smiled, seeing May standing on the porch with Mama Irene.

"I'm sorry it's so late," she said with a bright smile, "but Mama Irene thought it would be better if I came back here and slept. She said you have an extra room."

"Yes! I'm so glad you came back," smiled Mila. "Come in, come in. Thank you, Mama Irene."

"No problem, honey. Here, I brought some lemon squares. They're perfect for girl talk with some hot tea." She handed Mila the plate, and instinctively, she lowered her face, smelling the strong lemon. "Good night. Sleep well."

Mila shut the door, engaging the locks, and then turned to smile at May, who was already putting the tea kettle on the stove.

"Did you get all the gear you needed?" asked Mila.

"Yes, I had some already. I did an excavation in Peru a few years ago, so I had some cold-weather gear, but the man that took me to my apartment and brought me back insisted that I stop for more stuff."

"Who was it?" asked Mila, curious to know if it was Thomas or Bron.

"His name is Bull. He's with RP, but he is one scary man. I mean, he's super nice and gentle, but if I saw him walking toward me in a dark alley, I'd faint."

"I think that's the point," laughed Mila. "I noticed at dinner that they're all built like that. They have these stone faces with hard, angled cheekbones. Their bodies seemed chiseled from granite, and the smell of testosterone is everywhere. It's overwhelming, and I was an active-duty Marine at a base in Iraq. Believe me, I was surrounded by testosterone, but this is on a whole other level."

"Most of my colleagues are men, so I know what you mean. Twenty years ago, archaeologists were geeky, khaki-wearing nerds with glasses. Now, they all want to be Indiana Jones. They're muscular, tattooed, and in a university setting, they're rock stars. Some of them even have their own adventure shows or explorer blogs."

"I've seen those!" said Mila excitedly. "There's one, what's his name, Rock something or other."

"Rock Garvin. His real name is Richard Geller, but he thought a name change would be better for television," frowned May.

"Oh, you know him?" asked Mila as she set the lemon squares on two small plates, then thinking better of it, left them on the big plate. This might be an 'eat them all' night.

"I did. We dated for a while, about seven years ago, before he became famous. We were working on a dig outside of Jordan, originally searching for a king's burial site. What we found instead was a lost Crusader fortress filled with gold and jewels. It was a magnificent find."

"Wait, I watched that documentary with him in it, but I didn't see you," said Mila. Seeing the look on the woman's face, she understood. "Oh, shit."

"Yea, oh shit. He knew what we would find there. We'd been digging for days, and I was exhausted. I'd had a stomach bug for a few weeks and was finally getting to the point where I couldn't even hold down bread and water. He was trying to be really sweet, but I knew something was wrong.

"He convinced me to go into the city and get a nice hotel for a few nights. He kept telling me that a hot bath, a soft bed, and room service would make everything better. I had no reason not to trust him, so I did what he suggested. I took that hot bath and slept for twenty-four hours. When I woke, I ordered room service, turned the television on, and there he was, showing the cameras *his* find of the century. I wasn't mentioned, nor were any of the other members of the team."

"Wow, I'm so sorry, May," said Mila as she shoved the second bite of the lemon square in her mouth.

"Me, too. I gathered my things, left the dig site, and never heard from him again. Some of the other members of the dig team tried to sue him, but he was sneaky. Everything had his name on it. After that, someone convinced him he could make a killing doing these dumb television shows. He cut his hair differently, got both arms tattooed with full sleeves, trying to make himself look tougher than he really is.

"Hell, that man squealed like a little girl when a spider fell on his shoulder. He's not tough at all, just cunning."

"Sounds like we have lots of stories to tell," said Mila. May tilted her head in a questioning way. "As a woman in the Marine Corps, you're not exactly the dominant sex. Most of the men assume you're a lesbian, and if you're not, then you must be there to jump their bones. They're sadly disappointed when you don't want to do either.

"My experience wasn't exactly like yours, but whenever a tango was caught, or a kill made, my team made sure I didn't have any credit, even if it was all mine. I knew I was going to go to CID eventually. In an irony of all ironies, my first case was against a former teammate who lied about a capture and kill. He about shit his pants when he saw me enter that interrogation room. He'd lied about an incident that I was involved in.

"He knew his goose was cooked and immediately confessed. It wasn't how I wanted to win my first investigation, but it was worth it to see the look on his face."

"I don't get the sense that Thomas and Bron are like that," said May.

"No, I don't think they are," said Mila. "I think they're intensely protective of women, and of their teammates, in all fairness. I just wish that I could convince Bron to trust me. I wasn't completely honest when I first came asking for their help, but I have been since then."

"Do you mind if I ask you why you're doing this? I mean, Adele said that Lora was your roommate the last few years, but you pretty much left one another alone. If you weren't close, why risk your life for this?"

"It's a fair question," said Mila, taking another lemon square as May did the same. "I've never had a lot of friends, May. Especially female friends. I was the tomboy, and most of my friends were boys until they got to the age where they either wanted a girlfriend or a fuck-buddy. Lora was the first woman I'd ever met that was content to be my friend without being attached at the hip.

"When we were both available, we'd have dinner or coffee, sometimes go on bike rides or hikes together. But we weren't in each other's business. It surprised me when I found out she was dating Mike, but they seemed happy, really happy. That first trip they took, she came back looking depressed, and I thought maybe she'd discovered they weren't right for one another.

"Then, when they took the second trip, I knew something didn't feel right. She was a private person, but she always told me where they were going, and this time, she didn't want to tell me. When I found out they were going to China, I knew there was some other reason. Mike shouldn't have been allowed in the country. Maybe that's what they were waiting for in San Francisco. I don't know.

"All I know is, the only woman who was ever my true friend has been murdered, and I want to find out why and by whom."

"I hope to have you as my friend, Mila," smiled May. "I can't say I've ever had a female friend that would go to such lengths for me, either."

"Well, then," smiled Mila, "let's make a pact. I'll watch out for you. You watch out for me. If you need me to bury a body, I will." May laughed.

"I don't think I'll need you to bury a body, but I may need to have some girl chats on hopefully climbing a body. Thomas is mouth-watering in every way." Now it was Mila's turn to laugh.

"Yes, I can see that, although I have to say, Bron's body is what does it for me." She shook her head, licking the sticky lemon off her fingers. "He kissed me earlier tonight, and I won't lie, May, I thought I was going to orgasm in my jeans."

"Wow, that's a good kiss," laughed the woman.

"It was amazing, but he pulled back and apologized," she frowned.

"Ouch. Maybe he's just trying to keep his head with all of this. I mean, they're going to need to have a clear head as we get deeper into this thing."

"Maybe. Or maybe, he's not over his ex-wife like he professes. I don't know. I know Lora regretted leaving him. She always said he was the best sex she'd ever had," smirked Mila. "We'd been living together a few months when she talked a little about him. Lora said he was her youthful mistake. Hot Marine with a hot body and a cock that could rock her world. Her words, not mine. She admitted that they'd moved too fast, and she regretted getting married almost immediately.

"I guess he wrote to her all the time, tried to call her, but she just kept pushing away, thinking that if he couldn't talk to her, he would lose interest. It forced her to make the decision. He wasn't even fully inside the door of their apartment when she said she was leaving. He didn't fight her, from what she said. He signed the papers, and that was it.

"She left California for a while. She took a job at UNLV in Las Vegas and then from there went to UC Santa Barbara, which eventually led her back to UC San Diego. She knew that Bron was gone from the area and hoped she wouldn't see him again."

"That's sad to me," said May. "I mean, he goes off to fight for his country, and she's sitting there ignoring his messages. I can't imagine what was running through his head."

"I didn't say she was smart, but she did have regrets." They both stared at the empty plate of lemon squares and laughed. "Well, I guess we should get some sleep. We have to be at the airport by eleven tomorrow. I'm glad you're here, May."

"Me, too," she smiled. "I'm glad you're here as well. We're going to figure this out, Mila."

"I hope so. I really, really, hope so."

CHAPTER NINE

Mila and Bron were seated in 3A and 3B in first class, with May and Thomas across the aisle. They were holding hands, smiling at one another. The blush on their cheeks told anyone who walked by that they were into one another.

Bron stared at Mila's hand on the armrest. Her nails were neatly filed to an appropriate length, the pale blush polish perfectly glossy. Reaching for her hand, he gripped her fingers and brought her hand to his lips.

Mila turned sharply, staring at Bron. What was his game?

"Remember," he whispered, leaning toward her, "we're a young couple in love." His lips were just inches from her own, and she could feel her breathing quicken as he leaned further in. Gripping the back of his neck, she pulled him the rest of the way and kissed him, her tongue diving forward and tasting the warm coffee and beignets he'd had in the airport.

When she pulled back, he looked shocked and surprised, and Mila felt a personal victory in her chest. Somewhere over the north Pacific, Bron turned to her and kissed her again, this time without explanation.

"Tell me about your childhood," he asked. "You said you were an orphan."

"Oh. Yes, I was," she said with a shocked expression. "There's not a lot to tell. My parents abandoned me in the hospital. I was in an orphanage until I was six and then adopted."

"Yes, but you said the adoption wasn't ideal for you. Why?" he asked. Mila looked out the window of the plane, the blackness of night making seeing anything at all impossible.

"The family that adopted me, they adopted me for all the wrong reasons. Henry and Barbara Lambton were upper-crust society in Connecticut. They were expected to have children, lots of children. Unfortunately, neither of them knew the first thing about children and didn't really want them complicating their lives.

"I was six when they brought me home. I had two adopted older brothers. One who was already in college and drowning in cocaine. He died a year after I arrived. I only met him once."

"I'm sorry," said Bron, frowning at the woman. She just shook her head.

"My other brother and I tried to be good kids, tried to do what they wanted us to do, but they were so lost. Nothing was good enough for them. I'm not sure where Pete was adopted from, but I think he had some developmental issues, maybe Asperger's or something. I'm not sure. God, they were horrible to him.

"They weren't abusive, but then again, maybe they were. They were always putting him in situations that he just couldn't handle. He'd scream and cry, throwing things. Finally, they sent him to a boarding school somewhere in England. I didn't even know where he was. They wouldn't let me write to him. I tried to find him for years.

"As for me, I was everything they didn't want for an obedient daughter. I was defiant, smart, independent, and I wasn't a lily-white, blue-eyed, blonde-haired baby girl. I was darker, naturally from my heritage. My eyes were amber, not blue. Everything about me was wrong."

"There's not one damn thing wrong with you," growled Bron. She stared at him, swallowing hard as his stare cut through the fog of her brain.

"Th-thank you. When I decided to go into the Marine Corps instead of straight to college, they decided to disown me. I tried writing them, but they never wrote back. About three years ago, my adoptive mother died from a stroke, and a year after that, my father died of a heart attack. It shocked the shit out of me when their attorney said they left me an inheritance."

"Good for you," smiled Bron.

"I gave almost all of it away," she said with a nod. "I put enough into a savings that would ensure I'd be okay in any emergency. Paid off the house that Lora and I were living in, didn't tell her because I was afraid she'd move out. I liked having her there as my friend and roommate."

"That makes sense," said Bron. "A lot of guys have a hard time living alone when they come back from being cooped up with a bunch of men in a hut or tent somewhere." She nodded solemnly.

"Anyway, that's it. I don't know my real parents, have no clue where my adoptive brother is, and now it's just me."

"It's not just you, Mila," said Bron, still holding her hand. He rubbed his thumb over the back of her hand, and a chill raced up her spine.

"Are you Hispanic? Caribbean? What's your heritage? Sorry, it's just that you have really striking features," she said, staring at him.

"It's all good, baby girl," he smiled. Mila felt her heart skip a beat at the loving term. "My mother was mixed, her grandfather had been white, but her parents were both black. My dad was white, but I never met him. I don't know anything about him. I did a DNA test once, and it came back with Irish, Italian, African, Caribbean, Spanish, and just a smidge of Norwegian."

"Norwegian?" she laughed. "Well, that might explain your size. You're big like a Viking."

"You've noticed my size?" he smirked.

"Bron, it's kind of hard not to notice your size. I'm pretty average for the American woman, but you're huge!"

"There is nothing average about you, Mila," he said with a sincere expression. "You're beautiful, curvy, gorgeous, smart. You are so far above average it's not even funny." She swallowed, shaking her head.

"You don't have to say all of that. No one is around us," she whispered.

"I'm not saying it for anyone around us. I'm saying it for you because I mean it. I didn't react well to our kiss, Mila. The truth is, I've been feeling out of sorts lately, and about a week ago, at a double wedding at the RP compound, I got drunk and acted like an idiot. I'm ashamed of myself for that, but I did it because I've been missing something in my life."

"You have?" she asked.

"I have," he grinned. "I've been a Special Forces Marine for the last fifteen years, Mila. After my divorce, I just figured it wasn't a good idea to start another relationship. Lora was right. We were too young, and we moved too fast, but we were both feeling the need for something permanent in our lives. It was wrong.

"I knew that I wouldn't start another relationship until I was somewhere permanent. Now I am. I know that this isn't ideal, and starting a relationship under these conditions seems foolish, but I'd damn sure like to get to know you on this trip. I know we have a mission. I know we're trying to accomplish something, but nothing says we can't try to accomplish two things."

"Wh-what's the second thing?" she stammered.

"This." He slammed his mouth to hers, nibbling on her lips, stroking her jaw as his big hand slid behind her neck, tilting her head slightly to the side. She gasped for air, only allowing him to delve deeper into her mouth. Pulling back, she glanced down at his lap. The long thick cock was outlined against his dark trousers, and she felt the flood of warmth and wetness between her legs.

Bron was in pain. His cock was so hard, he needed to get relief, or he was going to be a miserable son-of-a-bitch for the remainder of the flight. He looked down at her chest, the taut nipples poking through the fabric of her t-shirt. He groaned, closing his eyes.

The airline gods were on their side as the lights dimmed, plunging the plane into relative darkness. Thomas and May had their seats reclined, their faces turned to one another, whispering. Mila reached for the big quilted blanket and spread it over the two of them, then she pushed the armrest up, ensuring no barriers between them.

Opening her legs, she let one fall over his knee. He stared at her with clouded desire. Unzipping his loose cargo pants, she pulled the thick, heavy cock from his pants, and he closed his eyes. Grabbing his hand, she guided him to her warm, wet opening, and he took over from there. Desperate for release, they stroked and rubbed, staring at one another until they were at the precipice.

Mila opened her mouth, letting out a long, slow, ragged breath. Her eyes closed with relief as the orgasm rippled through her body. She was shocked at the control that Bron showed. His hot cum oozing over her fingers as he stared straight at her face. Trying to not make a mess, Mila knew she only had one option.

Bringing her hand to her mouth, she licked her fingers, cleaning her hand completely. Reaching inside her bag, she grabbed a few tissues and dove back beneath the blanket to wipe him dry. His eyes never left her face. When she was done, he leaned forward and took her mouth once again, nibbling on those beautiful, lush lips. He let his big thumb stroke over her erect nipple, and she gasped against his mouth.

He pulled back, resting his forehead against her own, kissing her once more.

"This will be continued properly, Mila. I want you in a bed beneath me," he whispered into her ear. She nodded, feeling the heat of excitement fill her face. He kissed her sweetly. "Sleep. It's going to be a long night."

CHAPTER TEN

"Tell me about you," said May, lying on her side, staring at the handsome face of Thomas Bradshaw.

"Well, my mother was Russian-born but came to America as a young woman. She was at university when she met my biological father and fell in love. While he was at sea, serving aboard a submarine, it sunk, and he died. He never even knew that she was pregnant with me. His father was a mentor to my mother and an admiral in the U.S. Navy. Her father, my Russian grandfather, was a psychopath with visions of ruling the world.

"You already know I have a pretty high IQ," he smirked as she pretended to be shocked. "My grandfather thought he could use that to his advantage. My mother married a man she didn't love to please her father and, hopefully, to give me a stable home. Unfortunately, he was a puppet for her father. They plotted to kill her and kidnap me. Which they did."

"Oh, my God, Thomas, I'm so sorry," she whispered with a tear in her eye. He smiled, shaking his head.

"It's okay. I was only in elementary school, and my teacher was Jessica, Merrick's wife. He's a member of RP now, but back then, their SEAL team was in San Diego. She saw signs of abuse by my father and grandfather and brought me to the hospital. After that, Merrick and his team kind of took over. They hid me from my grandfather and eventually helped to kill him. My biological grandfather was notified and came to get me.

"I had a wonderful life with him and my grandmother. He had me in advanced classes, but he also made sure that I played baseball and went to scouting and birthday parties. He wanted there to be balance, and there was. About six months ago, I was kidnapped by a man who wanted to use one of my technologies. I was rescued by none other than the men who'd saved me as a child.

"I knew then that it was kismet. I was supposed to be with RP, not some think-tank for the government. The man that kidnapped me had pumped me full of some nasty drugs, so I was in a rehab facility for a while. While I was there, the RP team visited me often and got me into physical fitness. I was surprised at how easily it came to me."

"Yes, it appears it definitely worked," smiled May.

"Oh, yea?" laughed Thomas. She nodded as he leaned forward, kissing her sweetly, innocently.

"You're very handsome, Thomas," she whispered.

"And you're very beautiful, May. This mission will be the easiest assignment I've ever had. I look forward to showing China my beautiful girlfriend. What about you? Tell me about you?"

"Oh, well, my parents are typical Chinese immigrants. My father is a math teacher at a local high school, and my mom works as a piano teacher. I have an older brother who is a math professor at Notre Dame. I've just always loved old stuff," she grinned.

"When I was a little girl, my parents took us back to see our grandparents. They took all of us to visit the Great Wall and the terra cotta soldiers. It was amazing. I just kept thinking, what would it be like to uncover something that was centuries old? So, I got my PhD in archaeology and started working on digs.

"The last one I did was seven years ago. The man I was working with, we were dating, and he ended up taking all the credit for the dig find. I left, applied for a teaching role at Tulane, and never looked back."

"I'm sorry to hear that," said Thomas. "Did you kick his ass? Can I kick his ass?"

"No," she laughed, "and, yes. If we run into him, I'd love to see you kick his ass. You've probably seen him on television, Rock Garvin."

"I've seen him, and to be honest, May, I already knew. I wanted to know as much about you as I possibly could." He leaned closer, his big hand covering the entire side of her face. "You see, May Wong, I'm enchanted by you, and I plan to make you mine."

He kissed her again. This time, his lips lingered. His tongue probed as his hands skimmed her side, gently squeezing her small breast, then covering one buttock cheek.

"Y-your hands are very big," she smiled.

"They are," he grinned.

"I'm just curious..."

"Yes, it is," he smiled.

Taking her hand, he held it against his stiff, rigid cock, and she realized it was longer than her hand from heel to fingertip. Her eyes widened, and she felt the wetness flood her panties. He kissed her nose, then her lips again, and pulled back.

"Not here, not now, sweet May. But you can damn sure bet when I get you in a hotel room, we're going to explore one another. Sleep, honey. It's a long flight." He closed his eyes, and she couldn't believe he wasn't begging for relief. Her own body was on fire, and she desperately wanted to crawl beneath the blanket and find some way to release the tension.

Instead, she rolled over, stared at her friend across the aisle, and smiled. Mila winked at her, and May knew. They were two very lucky women.

CHAPTER ELEVEN

It was mid-morning the following day by the time they checked into their hotel in Beijing. Dropping their bags in the rooms, they all showered and changed, then headed out for the day. Mila had a camera around her neck, May with a big sunhat and sunglasses pointing to things like every other tourist in the city.

"We're supposed to meet the others inside the Forbidden City," said Thomas.

"It's only a short walk," said May. "There are Chinese military guards outside the city. You cannot photograph them; they will arrest you. I know that you will be, but remember to be very respectful of the buildings and grounds."

"Would the Forbidden City have been here during Kahn's rule?" asked Bron.

"No. It was built after his death. The construction was started in 1406 and took fourteen years to complete with millions of workers working non-stop around the clock. Many died during the construction, and their bodies were simply removed in carts.

"The City is actually a series of buildings that you have to walk through to get to the next. Who you were here to see would determine how far into the City you got. The Emperor and his wives and concubines were at the back of the City. It was home to emperors and the center of China's political universe until around 1912. In 1987 it was declared a World Heritage Site, and efforts were made to repair damage done by revolutions and political conflicts. Many of the artifacts were returned, but they're still missing thousands of pieces."

"It's amazing," said Mila, staring at the huge buildings. She looked down to see Bron's fingers linked with her own and smiled.

"Each building has a purpose," said May. "If you start at the main gate, or Meridian Gate, you'll then walk through the Gate of Supreme Harmony, then into the Hall of Supreme Harmony, on back to the Palace of Heavenly Purity, the Imperial Garden, and residences. On the sides are the Hall of Literary Glory, Hall of Military Eminence, Southern Three Places, Palace of Tranquil Longevity, and there are the corner towers and four more gates."

"It's really incredible, May," said Bron. "I keep seeing lions all over the place. Do they have significance?"

"Lions are important in Chinese culture. They symbolize strength, stability, and superiority. If you look at all of the lions guarding the buildings, there is always one on the left with a ball under his paw, and the other on the right has a small cub under its paw. Some say the one with the ball is the male, always playful. The one with the cub is the female, always nurturing. Others say the one on the right is female because she's always right." May smirked at her friends, and they laughed, nodding their heads.

"It's truly incredible," said Mila. "We don't have things this old in America, so it always makes me feel so insignificant."

"Across the street is Tiananmen Square," whispered May. She wasn't even sure why she was whispering, but she felt the need to be quiet. Bron frowned, staring over the gates toward the huge concrete square. He felt someone bump into him and was prepared to turn and fight. Instead, CC laughed at him.

"Sorry, man. Didn't see you there," he laughed.

"Be glad you're a big bastard," growled Bron, nodding at Fitch. "Where's Hiro?"

"I'm right here."

"Fuck!" muttered Thomas and Bron together. The girls both jumped, then giggled.

"Where were you?" asked CC.

"The woman at the Starbucks apparently thought I was Chinese, not Japanese. Fortunately, I speak a little of the language, so I was able to order her double whipped, no fat latte." He smiled at the group, shaking his head.

"Brother, I'm sorry you had to leave your new bride at home. How is she doing?" asked Bron.

"She's actually doing great," he grinned. "She's the strongest, most beautiful woman I know, no offense to present company."

"None taken," smiled Mila. "It's nice to see a man so in love with his wife. Have you guys heard or seen anything?"

"No," said CC, shaking his head, "but then again, we're a long way from the Great Wall. Just an FYI, we're going to head to the Great Wall with you guys, then take the train legally into Mongolia. Ace was able to get our passports outfitted with special Visas. We'll meet you close to the base of the mountain after that."

"We made dinner reservations tonight for the hotel restaurant," said Hiro. "We figured everyone would be jet-lagged. Your guide picks you up at 0700 tomorrow. We cancelled the original guide and the hotel near the wall. It's unnecessary. We're going to hitch a ride with you, telling him our guide left us behind. He'll gladly accept the cash we offer."

"What about our bags and backpacks?" asked Mila.

"They'll be dropped at a point further across the wall. Bron and Thomas have the coordinates," said Fitch. "We'll see you at dinner."

The foursome waved at their friends, nodding, then turned back to May.

"What now?" asked Mila.

"Anyone up for some souvenir shopping?" Thomas and Bron both groaned, but the women grabbed their hands, pulling them toward the shops down Wangfujing Pedestrian Street. The dozens of shops, food carts, restaurants, and souvenir stands had people yelling at passersby, offering the best deals of the day.

"There are too many fucking people," growled Bron. "This makes me very uncomfortable."

"Okay," said May, nodding, seeing the man's distress. "I agree. Come on, I know a shortcut to the hotel." She wove them through the small alleyways, and the further they got from the main street, the quieter it became.

"Are you okay?" asked Mila, rubbing his arm.

"Yea, yea, I'm okay now. It was just a lot," he said, looking back behind them. "There are so many people here, and it's just a perfect place for someone to jump us. We need to get back to the hotel."

By the time they were back in their rooms, it was late afternoon, and everyone was exhausted. They knew they were meeting the others for dinner, so they changed and headed downstairs to the restaurant. Their reserved table had Hiro, Fitch, and CC already seated, the two couples waving and hugging their long-lost friends.

"Everything is usually served family-style," said May. "These lazy Susans in the center of the table hold the food, and you just spin it until you find what you want. They'll keep bringing it, as long as you keep eating it, so just stop when you're done."

Apparently, the idea of no longer eating was lost on CC. He continued to eat whatever was put in front of him, never questioning what the food was. The waitress, a young girl, being prodded by her older counterpart, finally stepped over and cleared her throat.

"Sir, we ask that you are done," she said softly. CC looked at her and then at May, who asked the woman a question in Chinese, and she responded.

"CC, they would like for you to be finished. They feel you've eaten enough for five men," smiled May.

"Oh, sure. It was really good," he said. "I'm a big boy and like to eat." May smiled, telling the woman they were done. They left a large tip at the table, thanking the waitstaff and the cooks. Off to their own rooms, they wished one another well.

Thomas looked at May and knew she was feeling nervous about their sleeping arrangements. He showered and changed in the bathroom, then turned it over to her. When she came back out, he was lying on the floor with a pillow and blanket.

"Thomas, you don't have to do that," she said, crawling between the sheets. "I don't expect anything to happen between us. Not tonight, anyway. We're exhausted. Will you just hold me?"

Thomas smiled at her, nodding as he stood. She could see his semi-hard cock and smiled, a blush coming to her cheeks once again. All these elaborate, romantic plans rolled through her head. Ideas of how she would seduce him and have her way with the beautiful Thomas Bradshaw.

But once wrapped in his arms, she succumbed to exhaustion, not moving until their alarm woke them the next morning. So much for seduction.

"Are you tired?" asked Bron, staring at Mila. She'd showered, her hair still wet was twisted on top of her head.

"A little, but I'd like for us to talk if that's okay," she whispered.

He nodded, pushing back the covers, and patting the mattress beside him. She wore a pair of cotton pajama pants and a black camisole. It shouldn't have been sexy, but it damn sure was. Bron was trying to hide his hard dick, but it was becoming increasingly difficult.

"What did you want to talk about?" he asked.

"I guess I just want to be sure that you're not feeling guilty or something about Lora. I mean, you said you didn't have feelings for her or anything, but I don't want to start this and then realize that you're thinking of her, not me."

He nodded, smiling at her.

"Come here," he said, pulling her into his arms. He kissed her forehead, rubbing her upper arms with his big, callused hands. "Mila, Lora and I were never really in love. I think we were in lust but not love. We met, and it was like a firestorm. We were young, horny, and hot for each other. I had just come back from one deployment, and they were already talking about another.

"As a young Marine overseas, it's fucking lonely. You want someone back home that can talk to you, write to you. I should have found a pen pal; it would have been less trouble. I didn't love Lora. I didn't hate her, either. We were young and stupid.

"What's happening between you and me, it's a mature emotion that the man I was ten and a half years ago wouldn't understand. I noticed how beautiful you are the minute I walked into the boardroom. Your frumpy black suit and hair tied up didn't take away from that. But when I saw you come out of the bedroom with your hair down and those white jeans, baby, I was hooked."

"Just like that?" she said, looking up at him with a smile.

"Just fucking like that," he growled. "Now, I want to make sweet, slow love to you, Mila. I want to make you see stars, but if you're not ready for that, it's okay."

"No, I'm more than ready," she said, sitting up. She tossed her camisole over her head and shimmied out of her pajama bottoms. Pushing the sheet down, she smiled to see him completely naked. Straddling his hips, she gripped his thick cock and lined her body up to his, slowly sliding down his length as he stretched her, filling her.

"I am so ready," she said breathlessly.

"Fuck, baby girl, so am I," he moaned. "I need to take control, Mila." She nodded, and he flipped her to her back, quickly pushing her legs wide and burying himself inside her. Mila gasped, gripping his thick head of hair, moaning against his lips.

Bron took one of those beautiful nipples between his teeth and tugged, tasting, and sucking, flipping it with his tongue as she writhed beneath him. He needed the release, and so did she. He could feel her walls squeezing him, trying to drain him of his ache.

"Oh, fuck, Mila," he growled, "you're so fucking beautiful, baby. Damn, your pussy feels good."

"Oooh, dirty talk," she grinned. "Well, your cock is fantastic, so fill me up, Marine."

"Fuuuuuck!" he yelled.

His hips thrust forward, faster and faster, pounding against her hips and thighs as his balls slapped her ass. The wetness created by their passion spilled over both of them as Mila cried out, her nails raking down his ass cheeks and thighs. Bron's balls tightened, his abdomen shaking as his body released into hers.

Kissing her face, he continued to move inside her, his cock already hardening again. Mila just stared at his beautiful face, pinching his nipples, then reaching between them, rolling his balls between her fingers. Moaning, he gripped her shoulders and slammed his body violently inside her. Pulling her toward him, he sat her up, straddling his thick thighs as she rode him.

Her breasts bounced against his chest, her sensitive nipples rubbing against the rough hair. She grabbed a fistful of hair, latching onto his lower lip and tugging with her teeth as he continued to pummel inside her. His big hand stroked her ass cheek, then slapped it, causing the sensations to tingle throughout her body.

She felt his big finger rubbing around her tight, puckered hole, and she nodded.

"Yes, please, Bron, yes," she moaned.

"Fucking hell, baby girl, you were made for me," he said against her neck. His thick, long finger swirled around the tight opening, then entered her, his cock dancing inside her wet pussy.

"More, more!" she cried out.

Bron gladly stuck two fingers inside her and felt her immediate satisfaction roll through her body, shuddering, convulsing with release as he emptied himself into her once more. He slowly withdrew his fingers, gripping her ass again. She smiled, shoving him to his back and taking his cock in her mouth, her tongue wrapped around him, sucking the remnants of their love dry.

"We need to shower," he said, smiling down at her. She was lying on his stomach, her chin resting on her hands. He brushed a lock of hair from her face, the lust in her eyes already building. "Fuck."

Grabbing her hand, he pulled her into the shower, washing her as he got her ready for him again. He lifted her against the shower wall, throwing her legs over his shoulders while he buried his face in her pussy, his tongue moving in and out, around her sensitive flesh.

Gripping his head, Mila held him to her, praying he wouldn't let go. When she screamed her release once more, he bent her forward and slowly entered his cock into her ass. She'd had anal sex before but never really enjoyed it. Until now. Bron knew what he was doing and how to do it. He was amazing. Her tight ass strangled his dick, draining it of the last of his cum as she managed another orgasm.

Finally, back in bed in one another's arms, Bron turned to her.

"Listen to me, Mila. I don't know what happens after this, but I don't want this to end. I want you as mine, Mila. Mine. Do you understand me? I want you to be with me at Belle Fleur, in my bed every fucking night and every fucking morning. I want to wake up with my cock buried inside you, baby. I want to make you scream like that every damn day. Do you feel me?" Mila smiled at him, nodding.

"I feel you," she grinned. "I want that, too. I don't know how we do it, but I want it, too. I've never had an orgasm like I've had with you. Filling me completely, filling all of me completely, was beyond my wildest fantasies. You were made for me, Bron."

"Fucking right, I am," he grinned. "Now, go to sleep before I bury myself inside you again." Mila grinned, licking her lips.

"Oh, you think you have another one in you, Marine?"

"Baby, you're playing with fire," he growled. Mila pushed the sheets back, writhing on the bed.

"But I'm so hot down there," she moaned. "Please, Marine, please, help me, put me out of my misery." Bron tried to ignore her, he really did, but he just couldn't do it. He rolled on top of her, driving inside her, shoving his cock as far as her body would allow.

"Remember, baby girl, you asked for it."

CHAPTER TWELVE

Mila remembered his last statement from the night before as she tried to walk without discomfort. Everything on her body was aching from their exploration of one another's bodies. She'd always wanted adventurous sex, a little dangerous, and Bron was definitely the man to give it to her without judgment. Besides the fact that he was sexy as shit, his cock was huge, and he knew how to use it. She was sore, but she was happy.

"Did you sleep well?" asked May, smiling at her new friend. She damn well knew that they didn't sleep much. May and Thomas could hear them through the walls, making for some awkward and uncomfortable moments for them.

"Uh, well, I slept," she smiled. "Sorry, did we keep you up?"

"A little. It was fine. I fell asleep in Thomas's arms. I felt bad, but I was exhausted. I woke about three and heard you two going at it. Way to go, by the way." Mila laughed, shaking her head.

"He's incredible, May. I've never had a partner like him," she whispered. "I hope Thomas is the same for you."

"I have faith," she grinned.

"Good morning," said the guide. "We have a few other gentlemen that will be joining this private tour. I hope you don't mind."

"No, fine with us," said Bron, wrapping his arms around Mila from behind. He thrust his hips slightly forward, grinding his semi-hard dick against her ass.

"Really? Again?" she murmured.

"You started this," he whispered in her ear. She just laughed, shaking her head.

"Alright, if you'll follow me," said the guide. "My name is Xiang. I'll be your guide today, and I will point out several spots along the way that are significant in Chinese history. You will have plenty of time to spend on the Wall itself, so do not worry."

Xiang was true to his word. He talked nearly the entire way out to the Wall. He was thorough, informative, and according to May, factual.

"Alright, this is where you will begin your journey," said Xiang. "You can either take the lift up to the top and walk down, or you can walk up and then come down on the other end. Either way, I will be here waiting for you at four p.m. Take as much time as you need until then."

They waved at the guide and made their way to the lift, wanting to get there as soon as possible. It was crowded but still early, so the true crowds hadn't arrived. Making their way along the wall, they passed through several guard towers until they reached a low point in the wall.

Standing at the furthest precipice and the point which they thought would be the best drop point, May smiled at them.

"I guess I should have mentioned to you all that the Wall contains thousands of dead bodies of the workers. When they died while working, they were simply included in the wall with the mortar. It seems foreboding," she grinned.

"Are you trying to frighten us?" smirked Thomas.

"Nope, just telling facts."

Thomas took out his tablet, pointing it at the views in the distance, then turned and nodded to the others. He hit several buttons, and then CC moved forward, running the lines over the wall. Connecting the harnesses to Mila and May first, he carefully lowered the women over the wall, then watched as Thomas and Bron went.

"Tell him we took a taxi back," said Bron. "Let him know one of the girls wasn't feeling well. We'll meet close to the base of the mountain in two days."

"Be careful, brother," said Hiro. "The bags will be dropped in fifty-seven minutes at the drop point. Don't leave anything to chance."

Bron waved at his friends, releasing his own harness and hooking the others to the rope. CC dragged them all back up, tucked them in his backpack, then nodded at Fitch to release the camera freeze. They turned to see a guard walking toward them, not quite at the other guard tower yet. He was far enough away that he couldn't see what they were doing.

Turning in every direction, they pointed and laughed, then snapped a few pictures and began walking back toward the lifts. The guard waited for them, nodding as they passed him. They took their time, playing the role of tourist extremely well. CC stopped and bought several souvenirs, then they purchased some food from one of the trucks and sat at a picnic table and ate.

"Do you think they'll be okay?" asked Fitch. "That's a lot of fucking territory they have to cover, potentially all of it on foot."

"I think they have as good a chance as anyone. If I know Thomas, he'll invent some sort of device that will get them there in half the time. Or they'll hitch a ride. We'll be sure to be there for them," said CC. "Besides, from what I've seen of Bron, that's one stubborn bastard, and May has a vested interest in helping us find this."

"You got that fucking right," grinned Fitch. "Although, I never suspected Bron would fall in love."

"You think he's in love with Mila?" asked Hiro.

"Oh, I fucking know he's in love with Mila. I've seen that possessive look a time or two, and that bastard is done. Cooked. But I'll tell you this, I'm damn happy for him. When Lora dumped him like that, he was broken for a while. I don't think it was about love. It was about trust. He trusted her to be there for him, and she bailed the second it got hard. You all know that fear, which is why I suspect you didn't have relationships while in the service."

"You don't think they were in love?" asked CC.

"Nah. It was too fast, man. I was married to my first wife," he smirked. "I tried to talk him out of marrying Lora, knowing that it was just about being deployed and away from her for six months. I told him to give it the six months as a couple dating, then if she was there, marry her. But he got a taste of what she was offering and wanted to own it. They were young and stupid. We'd been on three back-to-back deployments and were headed for a fourth. He was lonely. Hell, all of us were. Lora was looking for a man in uniform, and Bron looked damn good in his. She was adventurous in bed, but she was a weak woman out of bed."

"That sucks," said Hiro. "It's why I never got serious with anyone while I was in the Army. I didn't want that happening to me."

"Yea, but you picked one that needed all the love and attention you could provide when you got out," smiled Fitch. "She's a keeper, Hiro, but a lesser man would have walked away from that precious woman."

"A lesser man would have been a fool," he smiled. "Winter is like this buried treasure. Every time I speak with her, touch her, something else is revealed, and she burrows deeper into my heart."

"Alright, boys, let's get to our ride and back to the hotel. We need to get to our other location by tomorrow night."

On the other side of the wall, four people were dodging between trees, traveling swiftly through the Mongolian forest. When they reached the drop point, four large backpacks were right where they should be. Two had tents tied to them. One had dig tools inside.

Each of them grabbed a backpack and, without a word, continued down their path. When they finally stopped for the night, temperatures were starting to drop. The men set up the tents, but no fire was created, just in case they were followed or being watched. Instead, they curled up inside the tent, waiting for morning.

CHAPTER THIRTEEN

"What do you mean they've taken a taxi back?" asked the driver. "This is highly irregular. They paid for a round-trip. I am responsible for their safe return!"

"It's alright," said Fitch, holding up his hands, trying to calm the man. "One of the women wasn't feeling well and wanted to get back sooner. I guess they didn't see you out here in the parking lot."

"Oh, well, I did leave to have lunch with my mother for an hour. She lives not far from here, and she's getting older now," said the man shyly.

Thank fuck, thought Fitch.

"It's all fine, really. They weren't upset at all. They just wanted to get her back to the hotel and rest."

The driver said nothing else, taking the men back to their hotel and offering them a ten percent discount on another tour. They thanked him but said they were taking the train to Mongolia the next day.

"Why would you go to that place? There is nothing of worth to see there," said the man. "Tourists, I will never understand you."

"What do you say we hit one of the restaurants on the next street over?" said CC.

"Sure," nodded both men.

The sheer size and stature of the men made heads turn. Although Hiro was the smallest, he was still a solid six-foot-one and almost two hundred pounds. It wasn't that there weren't big people in China, but most were on the small size. Staring at Fitch and CC was like looking at two American football players. The girls would giggle, whispering, and CC frowned, not liking the fact that he didn't understand their conversations and that they stood out from other men around them. It might make them easy targets.

The market street was busier at night than it was during the day. Locals and tourists alike flooded the street for food, souvenirs, and bargains. CC stopped at a large fabric shop specializing in Chinese silk, his huge hands skimming the delicate, intricate fabric.

"You got a fetish for silk, big man?" smirked Fitch.

"No," he laughed. "My mom likes to sew in her spare time. As a doctor, she's done her fair share of stitches, and she's really good. I was thinking about buying a few yards of this silk and taking it home to her."

"That's cool, man," nodded Hiro. "I'll bet she'd love it."

They stood over the table for several minutes discussing the colors and patterns, finally settling on a beautiful royal blue with Phoenixes flying across it. The woman nodded, taking their money, then speaking to Hiro in Chinese.

"What did she say?" asked CC.

"Well, I think she asked what was wrong with you? Why are you so big?" he laughed.

"Seriously? Brother, I'm a baby in our family," he laughed. The old woman laughed with them, grateful that the big American wasn't upset by her comments. "Tell her I like my milk." Hiro repeated the statement in Chinese, and the woman laughed harder. Reaching beneath the table, she handed another yard of silk to CC.

"She says this is a gift for the big, handsome American," smirked Hiro.

"Xiè xiè," said CC, surprising the woman with the Chinese word for 'thank you.' She laughed again, and the men went back into the streets to find something to eat. They laughed at the food carts with fried scorpions, chicken testicles, tuna eyeballs, and sheep penis. Snake soup, piping hot and ready to serve, along with other delicacies that Fitch wasn't sure his stomach was ready for.

They decided on a restaurant claiming to be the first to offer the famous Peking duck. Peking is the Romanized version of Beijing, although Fitch wondered why they didn't call it Beijing duck. Once again, they were faced with the infamous family-style dining and the lazy Susan.

"Now, remember, big man, when you're full stop, or they'll keep bringing more food," grinned Hiro.

"I hate to tell y'all this, but I wasn't full last night. I didn't want to stop. I got up and raided the mini-fridge in the middle of the night." It took two hours for CC to have his fill of the delicious duck and other delicacies put out. The waitstaff was attentive, friendly, and impressed by the men's abilities to use chopsticks.

Taking the shortcut back to the hotel, they wandered down the streets of Beijing. Small narrow alleyways, still cobblestoned from ages gone by. The mix of old and new all around them. Passing the last of the open businesses, Hiro pulled back on their shirtsleeves and signed to them.

"Three men up ahead."

CC nodded, looking at Fitch over Hiro's head. They continued to speak loudly, pretending as though they knew nothing. As they reached their turn toward the hotel, the three young men stepped out in front of them.

"Hello, American boys," said the one young man.

"We don't want any trouble," said CC. The young man looked up and up and up, finally landing on CC's sweet, kind face.

"Give us your wallets," he said, the switchblade gleaming in the dim light of the alleyway.

"And cell phones," said the other. Hiro smiled, taking out his cell phone spinning it on his fingers.

"Oh, you mean this?" He flipped it into the air, bouncing it off his knee and then kicking it high with his foot. It looked like a perfect score if he were playing soccer. The man eyed the phone as it sailed in the air, but unfortunately, took his eye off of Hiro, who spun, leaping into the air and kicking his cell phone directly at the man's face.

"Dude! You probably cracked your screen," smiled CC. "That's shitty."

The young man was howling in pain, his nose gushing blood into his hands. The other two men stepped out, one running toward Hiro. He took a step against the alley wall, attempting to come at him in a martial arts kick. Hiro ducked, his fist stretching upward, catching the man in the groin. He fell to the street, writhing in agony.

CC turned to the last man, his eyes darting from one man to the next. Before he could run, CC lifted him off the street, slamming his body against the wall as he gagged for air.

"You should learn to pick your victims more carefully," he growled. "Or better yet, get a fucking job and earn an honest living." He searched the young man's pockets, finding a wad of Chinese bills and tossed them to Fitch.

"Thanks for the extra cash," smiled Fitch. "Consider it payment for my friend's cracked phone screen. Drop him, big man." He tapped CC's arm, and the big man nodded, releasing his hold as the man got closer to losing consciousness.

Back at the hotel, they grabbed a drink in the hotel bar, smiling at one another.

"That was fun," smiled Fitch. "Although had the authorities come around, I feel certain we would have been charged, not our little friends."

"Do you think it has anything to do with why we're here?" asked CC.

"No," said Hiro, shaking his head. "They were thugs, waiting for someone to come down that alleyway. If it wasn't us, it would have been someone else unsuspecting, perhaps young women. Besides, only two were Chinese. The third was Filipino."

"Something to investigate on another day," said Fitch. "Bedtime, boys, we've got a long ride tomorrow."

"Awww, Dad!" yelled CC. All eyes in the bar turned, and Fitch moaned, shaking his head.

"Little shit, or should I say big shit. Get to bed."

CHAPTER FOURTEEN

Burkhan Khaldun loomed in the distance. Its peak still covered in snow and ice from the long winter. The entire area was protected by a national forest, but they were attempting to cross it unseen, anyway. The name Burkhan Khaldun means 'God Mountain,' and for May, she hoped it also meant that Kahn was buried there.

"I have to say, I'm not all that impressed with this place," said Bron, looking at the landscape. "It's pretty desolate and sparce."

"It's not much to look at," smiled May, "but it has great significance in the Mongolian culture. The history of the entire area is told in *The Secret History of the Mongols*. It's one of the most significant books ever written, particularly if you want to read about Kahn and his lineage."

"Then, my apologies," smiled Bron.

They'd been fortunate to catch a ride with a farmer who was driving to a nearby city. Otherwise, the walk would have taken them several days. They knew that the others would wait for them, but they weren't sure that Kahn's tomb would.

"Let's rest here," said Bron. "Mila? Where is that map again?"

"Here," she said, reaching into her pack and handing it to him. "I've looked at those drawings and maps so many times, my head just spins when I look at them again. I'm trying to understand why this was so important to them. She wasn't interested in history, and I don't think Mike was either."

"He definitely was not," said Bron. "Mike barely passed his tests to become MARSOC. I don't think he studied ancient Mongolian history in his spare time."

Thomas looked over his shoulder as they scanned the documents once again, pointing to the mountain in the distance.

"From this, it says we need to go to the northeastern side of the mountain, which could be challenging. Russia is located not all that far from here, and I'd like to not end up in a Russian prison if at all possible," said Mila.

"What is this?" asked Thomas, touching the surface of the intricate map.

"What?" asked Mila, staring at the paper.

"Here, these symbols. They're raised on the map," he said.

"I don't know," she said with a shocked expression. "I swear, I never noticed those before." May stepped closer, staring at the map.

"That's interesting. It's not a type of hieroglyphic, but it is something," she said, shaking her head.

"Oh, fuck," muttered Bron. "It's braille. This was put on the map at a later time. I have to get this back to RP. Bella is the only person I know that understands braille."

Thomas took out his phone, zooming in on the detailed dots, dashes, and lines. He sent it to corporate, copying Razor, hoping that his beautiful wife could help them. It was the middle of the night there, but someone would hopefully see the message and get back with them soon.

"Where are we meeting the others?" asked Mila.

"Hereleng Dugang," said Thomas. "It's a very small village that is typically housed by a nomadic culture of tribes. They have small campsites where climbers and hikers can stay, so I'm hoping they'll feel hospitable."

"What then?" asked May.

"We need to wait and see what these symbols tell us," said Bron. "Just because Kahn fought here and is thought to have died here doesn't mean this is where his tomb is located. We can't stay here forever, or we're going to create suspicion. Right now, we're just stupid, lost Americans. A week from now, we'll be considered something very different."

"What if this is all for nothing?" asked Mila. The others turned to stare at her. "I mean, what if this was all just some stupid game they were playing. Or what if they were seeking the treasure, not the weapon. What then? Do we just keep looking?"

"I think given the clue of a great weapon in their notes, we have no choice but to find it, baby," said Bron. "I know the tomb and treasure might be important for May, but it's not our first priority."

"Oh, I completely understand that," said May, shaking her head. "I don't think finding a treasure ranks with a potential new-age weapon. I'm not that narcissistic."

"You're not narcissistic at all," smiled Thomas, kissing her forehead. "You're a beautiful, intelligent woman who has a lot to offer anyone lucky enough to get your attention." May blushed, staring up at Thomas.

"And do I have your attention?" she asked, grinning at Thomas.

"You're damn right you do."

"Okay, love birds, what do you say we keep going and see if we can reach the village by nightfall?" smirked Bron.

Packing up everything they came with, they trudged further toward their rendezvous point. The ground was becoming harder, frozen, and sparse. The trees were fewer, which created issues if they needed to hide themselves. They were keeping a robust pace, moving without a lot of talking, stopping only for food or water, or to relieve themselves.

Reaching the small village just before dark, May asked for permission to camp, and it was granted. There were three other tents set up, and Bron noticed the familiar faces, nodding as if they didn't know one another.

"How long have you three been here?" he grinned.

"Train arrived about fifty miles from here around noon. We were told the hostels and hotels had been closed down about a year ago, so we bought some camping equipment. We took a taxi out this way, or at least, I think it was a taxi. There's nothing else after this. We did request some horses, but so far, they've been reluctant to grant our request," said Hiro.

"We have been invited to dinner, though," smiled CC. "I'm not sure what they're cooking, but it smells good to me."

"It's most likely ox, yak, sheep, or goat," smiled May. "You'd be surprised how flavorful it is, and it contains a tremendous amount of protein and much-needed energy for our hike tomorrow."

"Do you think they know why we're here?" asked Bron.

"I don't think so," said Fitch. "Hiro was able to speak with them and explain we were just a hiking team, trying to prepare for a race that was on similar terrain. One thing we have to be very careful of is the border."

"We were saying the same thing," grinned Thomas. "I do not want to have to explain to Cam and Luke why we need a prison break."

Looking up, they saw an older man coming towards them down a dirt road. He stopped in front of Hiro and May, obviously knowing that they were the only ones who might understand him. He spoke rapidly, his hands going in big circles.

"What is he saying?" asked Bron.

"There's a big storm coming. They've secured the livestock, but we can't be out here. He says they expect winds upwards of seventy miles per hour. There will be lots of snow. It's an unusual spring storm, but we can't avoid it," said May.

"What are we supposed to do now?" asked Thomas.

"He's offering us a room in his home. He and his wife are older, but they have a spare room where their son used to sleep. He thinks we can all fit," she smiled. The old man stared at CC, Fitch, Thomas, and Bron. "He hopes we can all fit."

"Alright," said Bron, "gather the gear and follow him. May, please thank him for us. Tell him we can pay him."

"It's insulting to offer payment, Bron. If it appears they don't have enough, we'll offer some of our food or other services."

Gathering their gear, they followed the old man along the dirt road, the winds already whipping at their backs. Mila shivered, realizing despite her top-of-the-line gear, this was going to be a bitter storm. The small house was the third in the line of homes along the dirt road. Stepping inside, they set their gear down and smiled at the old woman standing at the stove. May spoke to them once again.

"Thank you for your gracious hospitality for my friends and I." She bowed slightly to the woman, and she grinned a toothless grin. She pointed to the small room, and the men just smiled. They would barely fit sideways in the room, but if each lined up in the sleeping bags on the floor, they would be warm and safe.

Fitch and CC looked at the small woodpile and nodded to Hiro.

"Ask them where the wood is that we can cut," said CC.

Hiro did as they asked, and the man said there were logs behind their home but that he hadn't been strong enough to cut them. Fitch, Bron, CC, and Thomas went outside, bundled up against the cold. Thirty minutes later, they were piling stacks and stacks of wood in the bin and along the wall. It was enough to keep them for at least a few months. The old woman laughed, clapping her hands, and kissed the face of each man.

Hiro stood with her at the stove, asking about her recipe for yak stew.

"Do you think we could ask them about the mountain and the tomb?" asked Mila.

"We can try, but they may be extremely protective of it," said May. "You have to remember, he's considered a liberator, a hero, here in Mongolia."

"Anything could be helpful," said Bron. "It might be worth a try."

"Alright, I'll ask them a very benign question." Speaking in Chinese, she asked if they could tell them the story of Kahn and where he died. The husband and wife had an excited look on their faces, nodding at the group of interested people. They spoke as May and Hiro interpreted.

"Long ago, the land was divided among the Naimans, Merkits, Tatars, Khamag Mongols, and Keraites. The tribes fought often. Temüjin offered himself as an ally. A shaman determined that the world was set aside for him and only him."

"Whoa," whispered Bron.

"Temüjin gathered a massive army to defend the lands and began to attack instead of defending. He was victorious at every battle. Being the generous leader that he was, he gave authority based on the merit of those that followed him and their loyalty. As an incentive for absolute obedience, Temüjin promised wealth from future war spoils to his soldiers and people. When he won a battle, he did not drive the losers from their homes. Instead, he took them beneath his expansive wings and protected them as his family."

"This is not what I remember from history," murmured Fitch.

"Shush," said the old woman, nodding at her husband to continue. Fitch blushed, apologizing to the woman.

"His own mother would adopt the war orphans making them part of his family. The people were loyal, and with each victory, he became stronger. Other tribes pledged to fight for him. Some betrayed him. The great Khan died in the summer months. He told his men to bury him, there on our mountain," said the old man, pointing to the mountain in the distance. "It was to be kept secret so that his treasure would remain buried. He warned that if it were found and opened, there would be a surge of light like no other, and all in the world would die."

"What the fuck?" muttered Fitch.

"Are we talking nuclear-type reaction?" asked Bron.

"I'm not sure," said May. Turning to the old man, she asked him several questions. "He doesn't know. You have to remember that they are only repeating what legend has told them over the last eight hundred years. I mean, I can only imagine how those stories have become more fantasy than anything else. This could all be a way to keep us away from the tomb."

Ominously, the wind howled outside, rattling the boards of the old wooden house. The woman frowned at her husband. He stood, telling May that he was done. The woman scooped out bowls of the hearty stew and was pleased when the men returned for more.

"Ask her if she would like for us to replace the meat we've eaten," said CC. May nodded, asking the woman, and she laughed.

"They have yak in a pen at the end of the street," she said. "She thanks you, but it is better for her heart to watch you eat the stew."

"Tell her it's very good," smiled Bron. The woman smiled, grateful that someone was there to eat her meal. With no signal to contact the team back home, they were forced to turn in early. Although none of them complained.

Every hour or so, one of the men would rise and place another log on the fire so that the old man and woman could sleep through the night. The sleeping bags were lined up like soldiers in the tiny room. The team huddled together to keep warm. When sunlight filtered through the walls, Bron rose to open the shutters. The ground was covered in snow, but it was passable.

The old woman was already up and preparing breakfast for them. When they thanked them for their hospitality, Bron handed the old man a knife as a gift. He stared at it with eyes wide. He told May that he'd never seen such a fine knife and then asked a question.

"Uh, he's wondering if you have killed men with this knife," she said quietly. Bron stared at May, then Mila. Turning to the old man, he nodded.

"Tell him I had to kill enemies of my people, my tribe. I protected those that belonged to me," he said. She repeated what he said, and the old man nodded, speaking again.

"He said that Kahn would be proud of you. You would have made a great warrior for him."

Bron didn't want to tell the old man that he wasn't sure he could have fought for Kahn. After all, it was eight hundred years since the man had walked the earth. Did anyone really know what he was like?

The old couple waved at the group as they stepped outside, only to be greeted with seven horses. May smiled, turning to the old man, and hugging him and then his wife.

"When we are done with them, he said to set them free, and they will return home if we do not come back this way."

Happy to be off their feet for the day, Mila and May realized that their asses would be killing them by the end of the day. Still, it was a nice relief to have. Traveling in the snow would be hard, and it would be even harder on foot. At least this way, they could make it halfway to their destination today.

Around midday, they stopped for a small meal of dried meats and fruits that the old woman had given them. Thomas withdrew his tablet, trying to connect to the RP satellite. Finally getting his signal, he checked their messages.

"Hey, guys? We have a reply from Bella on the braille. It's a note from Mike and Lora. She said it reads, 'I hope you are seeing this and understand, Mila. Find Bron Jones, my ex-husband. He will help you. The tomb is not located where others suspect. They are after it and must not find it. You must travel across the national forest to Dadal, a lake on the Russian border. You will find it beneath the…"

"Beneath the what?" asked May.

"Beneath the head of the horse?" said Thomas. "What does that mean?"

"I have no idea, but this changes everything. If we have to cross that forest, it's going to take several days. Does it say anything else?" asked Mila. Thomas shook his head. "Damn! How do we know we can trust them? What if they're lying?"

"Why would they leave you that message if they were lying? I mean, why not just leave it in English if they were trying to fool you?" said Bron. "I think we need to consider this."

"It makes sense," said May quietly, perusing the map. "Kahn conquered that area and crossed into Russia many times to conquer other countries. Perhaps it was special to him for some reason. Maybe it was the home of one of his favorite wives or concubines."

"What do we do?" asked Mila pleadingly, staring up at Bron.

"We go to Dadal. We have no choice."

CHAPTER FIFTEEN

"What do you think?" Luke asked Cam and Eric. The two men were seated across from him in the quiet cafeteria. The breakfast crowd was gone, lunch not yet in full swing. They sipped their coffee, and Cam shoved his hand through his hair, causing his teammates to grin again. He stopped midway, realizing what he was doing.

"Fuck it, I can't help it. It's obvious the old man gave me his DNA," smirked Cam. "I'm not sure we should do anything other than be ready to pick them up if they get into trouble. I asked Adele to look into Kahn and the legends surrounding his tomb. The only thing she can find is something about gold and jewels, nothing about a weapon."

"I fucking hate to think of what they might find out there," said Luke. The door opened, and Ian, Marc, and Parker came toward them. The look on their faces said this was not going to be a happy conversation.

"What now?" asked Eric.

"The boys in the tech room heard some chatter about an archaeological dig and thought maybe our team had been found out. Except it wasn't our team. The buzz is that Rock Garvin and his team think they know where the lost tomb of Genghis Kahn is located."

"Oh fuck, no," said Cam, shaking his head.

"Do we have any idea where they're headed?" asked Luke.

"Somewhere in Mongolia. That's all we know. The chat room said that their location would be kept secret, but that Rock and his team had solid evidence of where the tomb was located," said Parker. "Now, the good news is we got hold of the documents found in the hotel room where Lora and Mike were found."

Marc took the papers and spread them on the table.

"If you look here, they created a number of entries in a journal citing that they had solid evidence of the tomb being found near Ulaangom on the western side of Mongolia near Russia. Legend has it that Kahn was in love with a princess of the region and wanted her for himself. He visited many times, but her father would not give the girl to him."

"Smart man," mumbled Luke.

"Maybe. The entries here say that Kahn got tired of waiting and took sixty thousand troops to take the tribe. The princess, on their wedding night, had a small knife on her and killed Kahn."

"That goes against everything that May told us," said Eric, frowning.

"It does, but there's always been a story out there about this. I found a book in Mama Irene's library about the history of the Mongols, and it was suspected that he'd been killed by a princess who didn't want to be his wife. Most historians refused to believe that, thinking that Kahn was too smart to be killed by a woman. Now, we all know that we have some damn smart women here who are more than capable of killing our asses, so it doesn't seem far-fetched to me."

"Okay," said Cam, standing and pacing around the table. "Let's assume that Lora and Mike were, in fact, trying to keep the tomb out of anyone's hands that might use this secret weapon. What if they created these journals to throw them off?"

"It's possible," said Luke. "I think the bigger question is whether or not Garvin is capable of killing to get what he wants. If he is, we need to send help to our team."

"That might be a good idea," said Marc. "Garvin travels with about forty to fifty people at all times. Seven are designated as security. He petitioned the Mongolian government to allow him to bring in weapons to protect the dig site."

"Did they give him permission to dig?" asked Luke.

"Not really," said Parker. "They gave him permission to explore the area. If he believes he's found the tomb, he must let the government know, and they will decide whether or not he can dig. But this guy leaves a trail of lies and suspicion behind him. It's not just the dig where he took credit from May, but he's done it several times to other archaeologists."

"I think this guy lets others do the work, and then he takes the credit," said Ian. "It might also interest you all to know that every dig he's ever been on, dead bodies turn up. And not old dead bodies. New ones. He's seen as reckless, ruthless, and without an ounce of honor. No one wants to work with him any longer, except the television network that produces his show."

"Is that where he's getting the money for his expedition?" asked Eric. The others all nodded. "I wonder. What if the network were suddenly slapped with an FCC investigation? That might force them to pull back a bit on his excavation, at least until we can decide whether or not our site is the right one or this one."

"I'll have the legal team get to work on that. Send in a few more men, five or six, just in case they need support. Drop them by air, and for fuck's sake, avoid Russia," said Cam. "What else on the evidence from the murder scene? Anything?"

"Yes," said Ian. "There was no mention of a potential weapon in these notes. I'm not sure whether that was intentional or not, but I'm concerned that our notes could be fake as well."

"How the fuck do we find that out?" asked Luke.

"Well, here's a thought," smiled Parker. "What if we backed a dig by another group? I mean, we could send a group of our own archaeological team, beat Garvin to the punch, so to speak. While the network is tied up with the FCC, and he's sitting there with his thumb up his ass, we send in a rival."

"Who, besides May, has he pissed off?" asked Eric.

"Donald Roth. He's a professor of archaeology and a recognized explorer by that big national magazine. Garvin stole a find from him in Peru a few years ago. Despite being warned by May and a number of other people, Roth agreed to work with him. Apparently, Garvin got some of the men to tell Roth that the lost city was located further south, and he sent him on ahead, citing Montezuma's revenge.

"When Roth got there, it was nothing but a blank canvas of farmland. It took him four days to get back to the site where Garvin was already giving interviews and filming. Roth knew what had happened, and he left, never speaking of it again."

"Give him a call," said Cam. "Tell Dr. Roth everything, so he doesn't think we're trying to screw him over. In fact, tell him this is payback for what Gavin did to him."

"Who do you want to send to Mongolia?" asked Parker. Cam grinned at the big man, eyeing his prosthetic leg.

"How's the leg feeling?"

"Like it's my own," grinned Parker.

"Good. You three go, along with part of Team Big. You, Noah, Noa, Frank, and just because I don't want to hear them whine, Alec and Tailor." The men all chuckled.

"This is going to be so much fun," smiled Ian. He looked up to see the groups coming in for the midday meal and spotted Alec and Tailor, connected at the hip as always. He nodded to Cam as the table watched him speak to the two older men.

"Are you serious? You're not messin' with me?" said Tailor.

"Yes!" screamed Alec. "I'm going to pack!"

"What about lunch?" asked Tailor, looking confused.

"Right. Lunch first, then we pack. We get to go on a trip!" Ian smirked at the table of his leaders and shook his head.

"Fucking children. I work with children."

CHAPTER SIXTEEN

"Yea, we read you, Cam," said Bron. "Sounds good. We'll keep going in our direction. You just keep that prick Garvin away from us. We have a few more days ride before we get to the lake, but we're hoping we can make good time tomorrow."

"Be careful, brother," said Cam. "You're going against what the Mongolian people want, plus now you're fighting this egocentric bully, Garvin."

"When will Roth get to the site?" asked Bron.

"He should arrive by tomorrow evening with Tailor and Alec. Garvin is stuck in Seattle pending the okay from the network. Kat and Katrina did a good job of sending the FCC after them. They're shitting in their pants right now."

"Good," nodded Bron. "That will give him a chance to set up his dig site. Garvin will shit his pants if he tries to bully those two."

"That's the hope, brother. That's the hope. Be careful."

Bron ended the call, staring into the darkness. Behind him, the team was huddled around the campfire, the smell of meat wafting through the cold air. He smiled as the beautiful form of Mila walked toward him.

"Everything okay?" she asked, wrapping her arms around his waist. He turned her, leaning her against the tree behind them.

"It is now," he smiled, grinding his hips into her.

"Oh, please," she whispered. "Bron, we can't. Everyone is right over there."

"It's pitch black. No one can see us, baby girl. Besides, it's too fucking cold to get naked. But it's not too cold to handle things for you." He cupped his hands over his mouth, warming his fingers up. Sliding his hands down her woolen leggings, he lay his big hand over her sex, one long finger entering her wet, hot channel.

"Oh, God!" she murmured.

"Shhh, baby girl," he whispered. "Don't let them think you're hurt and come running. This is practice. Let's see if you can cum nice and quiet."

She nodded as his fingers scissored inside her, his other big hand squeezing her breasts, tweaking her nipples. His mouth covered hers, swallowing her screams as she came all over his fingers. Bron removed his hand, licking his fingers as he smiled down at her.

Mila grinned up at her big hunk, then unzipped his pants, kneeling before him. He wanted to tell her no, that it wasn't necessary, but fuck, her mouth felt so good wrapped around his cock. One slender hand stroked him as she sucked his head. The other cupped his balls, rolling them gently back and forth.

Gripping her hair, he thrust forward, filling her mouth with all he had to offer. Mila swallowed, licking her lips, then cleaned his cock, kissing his balls. She heard the low rumble in his chest and smiled.

"Fuck, woman, that was awesome," he moaned against her lips. She nodded, but he noticed the wetness in her eyes and pulled back. "What's wrong?"

"Nothing. Nothing is wrong. I guess... I guess I'm just scared, Bron."

"Scared of what, baby? I'm not leaving. I'm right here."

"What if this weapon is real? What if all of you are risking your lives for something we should stay away from? What if when all this is done, you decide that I should go back to San Diego and stay?"

There it was. That was the one that was really bothering her. It didn't matter how much they made love, how much he talked about a life with her. She wouldn't believe it until it happened.

"Listen, Mila, I know that you don't know me all that well, although it damn sure feels like we've known one another a lifetime. But I don't lie, ever. I've never in my life lied to a woman. If I fucked a woman, keyword being fucked, not made love to her, I told her it was a one-time thing.

"I know that you have a life and career in San Diego, but I'm damn sure hoping that you can find your way clear to have a life with me at Belle Fleur."

"Really?" she asked quietly.

"Baby, what did you think we were doing this past week?"

"Fucking?" she shrugged.

"No. Well, yes, technically, we were fucking, but it was laced with love, baby girl. We were making love to one another and making memories. I'm crazy about you, Mila. I want us to try and have a life together."

"Yea?" she said, wiping the tears in her eyes.

"Yea, baby."

"Okay. We'll figure it out, but I'm still worried about what we'll find out there or worse, who we'll find out there."

"Let's let May figure all that out."

"You guys okay out there?" called CC.

"We're good. Nature called, and all that bullshit," said Bron, grabbing Mila's hand walking back to the fire. He repeated what Cam told him, and May frowned, shaking her head.

"He's trouble," she said, frowning at the group. "If he gets into Mongolia, we'll be racing against him and the clock."

"We think he's headed to the other site on the side of the mountain, May," said Bron. "We won't let him get in the way of us or Dr. Roth. Our teammates will make sure he's protected."

"That's good to hear. Roth is a good man. He's been doing this for forty years and has only made some minor discoveries. He deserves to have a big one all to himself." She stood, wiping her hands down the front of her pants. "I'm just going to walk for a minute and clear my head."

"Not alone," said Thomas, standing beside her. The others smirked as Thomas held her hand, walking into the darkness.

"Those two do the deed yet?" asked Fitch, grinning.

"Not yet," smiled Mila, "but the night is young."

May was quiet as they walked a few hundred feet away from the camp. There was the danger of a stray snow leopard or another mountain cat, but they were rare in this part of the country. Spotting a fallen tree, she took a seat, and Thomas sat next to her.

"All I've ever wanted, my entire life, was to discover something that no one else alive had seen. I wanted that moment when you open the tomb or the box and something magical stares back at you, letting you know that you're among the luckiest in the world to have seen it."

"You may get your wish, honey," said Thomas, tucking her hair behind her ear.

"Are we dating?" she asked, staring at him. Thomas chuckled.

"I'm not sure anything we've done could be considered dating. We've slept together without being intimate. We've ridden horses together across the Mongolian landscape. We've traveled together. We've kissed. We've touched."

"Do you want to date me?" she asked.

"I want to do a lot more than date you, May," he said with a white cloud of cold breath. "I want to make love to you in every way a man and woman can." May stood, unzipping her jeans. She reached for Thomas's zipper, and he gripped her wrist.

"Are you sure?" he asked. She nodded as she pulled his rigid cock from his trousers. Even the blast of cold air couldn't deflate the thick, hot piece. Her eyes got big and round, and he grinned. "I'll be gentle."

Thomas turned, straddling the log and laying back as she straddled his body backwards. She placed her feet between his legs, not wanting to remove all of her clothes. Crouching above him, she lowered herself onto his steel pole and simply glided downward, the feeling of satisfaction racing through her body.

When she was fully seated, Thomas sat up, gripping her knees as she raised and lowered herself on him. Reaching beneath her jacket, he massaged her small, delicate breasts as her breathing quickened. She stood quickly, kicking off one boot and removed one leg from her pants, then facing him, straddled him again.

"I need to kiss you," she whispered.

"Fuck yea," he muttered.

Wrapping her legs around him, she ground herself onto him. It felt as if she were back on the horse she'd ridden all day. Strong, powerful, demanding. Thomas took control, his rough thumb pad rubbing her sensitive hard numb. Covering her mouth with his own, he felt her shake and shudder beneath his touch, then his hot cum filled her seconds later.

"We didn't use a condom," she smiled.

"I don't care," he grinned. "I'm fucking crazy for you, May."

"Me too. I mean, I'm crazy for you. I'm not worried about babies. I'm on birth control. I was more worried about disease."

"Oh," smiled Thomas, feeling himself harden inside her once again. "I've never gone unprotected before. I haven't been with anyone in almost a year. I'm clean. RP requires testing, and I'm clean."

"Okay," she nodded, slowly rocking against him again, "me too. I mean, I'm clean too. Oh, God, Thomas, you feel so good. You're so big."

"You're so fucking small and perfect," he growled. "Ride it, baby. Cum for me again."

When May climaxed again, they stood and dressed. Thomas watched her walking back to the fire and smiled to himself. Fifteen-year-old, nerdy, no girlfriend Thomas would love looking at himself now.

CHAPTER SEVENTEEN

"I don't believe I've ever met two men, who were larger than you two," smiled Dr. Roth. "Of course, I'm on the small side of the gene pool, which is why I chose academia."

"Well, sir, maybe we're a study for someone along the way," smiled Tailor. "It's not the first time we've been stared at for our size. The truth is, sir, there are a few dozen more like us back home."

"You know, this seems appropriate that you're here. There was a four-thousand-year-old skeleton found near here. They called him the Longshan Giant. He was the tallest ancient skeleton found here, and he was only six-feet-three," smiled Dr. Roth.

"Maybe we're related," grinned Alec.

"I do believe you might be a species all your own, young man," laughed the doctor. "Are we certain that Garvin hasn't beat us to the site? He can be quite ruthless when he's focused on a dig or a find."

"We're positive, sir. He's still being held on the ground in Seattle. We have at least three days' head start on him. I'm hoping you can use this map to start digging. If it's real, wonderful. If it's not, then maybe May and the other team can find something."

"I truly hope she finds it," said Roth. "She's a lovely young woman, and that man was awful to her. He doesn't care about the archaeological find. He cares about the publicity, the book signings, and the television deals. He's a disgrace to our profession."

"Well, sir, we'll take care of him. You just tell these boys where to dig, and we'll watch out for any trouble." Alec smiled at the big man, and he nodded.

Roth took control of the site immediately, setting up tents and excavation areas. Using the LIDAR technology that his friendly giants brought with them, he scanned the area, allowing them to review the data with him when he was done.

He wasn't sure how they'd gotten permission so quickly, but he wasn't going to argue with it. Using the map left for them, he gave directives and then sat back, waiting and hoping.

"It shows that something is definitely beneath the hill," said Alec. He pointed to the screen, and Dr. Roth nodded, smiling at the two men. "You can see the outlines of man-made square structures. You see, these are rough, like a rock or boulder, but these here, they're definitely man-made."

"It's a temple," he said quietly. "I can't believe it. It's a temple usually built for those of great wealth or prominence, or perhaps for a Buddha. It might house his tomb as well, or it could simply be a buried temple. Either way, we've found something wonderful, gentlemen."

"Well, now you know where to dig," smiled Tailor. "You dig. We'll guard."

"Deal," laughed the older man.

"What the hell is that?" asked Mila, pointing to the sky. They all looked up, Bron the first to grin.

"That, my baby, is a group of RP men, better known as Team Big, coming to lend a few big hands. Let's go. Ha!" he called to the horses, snapping the reins. The others followed, galloping toward the men falling from the sky. They landed on the edge of the lake, expertly folding up their chutes as they walked toward the horses.

"Nice horses," smirked Noa.

"Nice parachutes," grinned Fitch.

"Holy hell, they're huge," whispered May. Noah raised his brows, staring at the woman, then grinned.

"We will not harm you, May Wong. We are here to help you with this excavation. I am Noah Anders. This is Noa Lim. I am No-ah. He is Noa. Frank Robicheaux, Ian Robicheaux, Devin Parker, and Marc Jordan." May nodded at the big man, the crisp tone of his speech making her smile.

"Can I study them?" she asked, leaning toward Thomas. Thomas let out a big belly laugh as the men shook their heads.

"Any luck so far?" asked Ian.

"We haven't even started to rope off the area," said Bron. "We were just arriving when we saw you guys dropping. We're looking for a site that's below the head of the horse, whatever the fuck that means."

Noah tilted his head, smiling at something as the others looked in his direction. The men knew what was happening, but Mila and May were confused. He nodded several times.

"It is a rock in the shape of a horse's head," said Noah. "What you're looking for is beneath that rock."

"Wait, how did he know that?" asked Mila.

"Well…"

"I speak to the dead," said Noah plainly. "Specifically, I speak to dead children whose souls, for whatever reason, are still here."

“We really need to work on your delivery, brother,” said Ian. Noah frowned, staring at the women.

“Did you not understand me?” he asked with a frown, looking toward May and Mila.

“No, no, I understood you,” said Mila. “You said you think you can speak to dead people.”

“I don’t think it. I can.” Mila stared at the big man, then looked back at May, who shrugged her shoulders. “There is a child here now. She died during the Yuang dynasty and knows the legends around the great king.”

“That was the dynasty almost immediately after Kahn’s death,” said May.

“She says the place you seek is a rock over that way,” he pointed. “Once, the lake was lower, and the rocks were higher. She said this used to be a cliff. The rock you seek is shaped like a horse’s head, and there is something important buried behind the rock.”

The team looked at one another, unsure of whether to head to the rock or not. Noah stared at them, wondering why they weren’t moving. Then, Bron stepped forward, holding the reins of his horse.

“Let’s go. I doubt a seven-hundred-year-old little girl would lie to us.”

They walked around the banks of the vast lake, Thomas looking at the maps on his tablet, realizing how very close they were to the Russian border. Reaching the rock, they stepped back and stared at the massive granite enclosure. The naturally occurring figure of a horse’s head was difficult to see at first.

“His nose is here,” said Bron, touching the tip of the rock. “Look. Follow it up to the ears, then back to the mane. It’s a head. It’s not carved, but it’s natural in the rock. A few hundred more years, and it might not be visible to anyone.”

"How do we get the rock out of the way?" asked Hiro.

"We have to move it," said Noah, looking down by his side. He nodded several times, and the women just smiled, realizing that perhaps they didn't know everything. "The child says it will take all of us and a lever."

Parker looked around the lakeside, seeing several downed trees. He pointed to one that looked as though it might work. He and Ian carried it back to the rock, prying the edge beneath the lip on the side of the rock. The women stepped back as the men began to push against the rock.

At first, there was no movement whatsoever. Frustrated by the use of the lever, they pushed it aside and simply began to move their weight and muscle against it. A loud creak gave way, stopping them to be sure they weren't damaging the rock face. Bron nodded at them, positioning themselves once again to move the boulder.

With a heavy groan, the rock rolled to the left, the men using the momentum to push again until a wide opening of a cave came into view.

"Fucking hell," muttered Frank. "It's a damn cave."

"No," whispered May. "It's a tomb. It's intentionally carved into the rock."

She stared at it for a moment, unable to believe it was real. Reaching into her backpack, she retrieved the large flashlight and shone it inside the dark space. Immediately inside was a flat rock surface for a floor, surrounded by paintings and markings. Directly in front of her was a long stone staircase leading to the chambers below.

"What does it say?" asked Mila.

“It tells the story of the great king, the one and only ruler of the earth and the sky. It shows his conquests, his victories in battle. It’s basically telling his life story, but it’s not giving his name. I think we have to assume it’s Kahn.”

“What’s this?” asked Mila, pointing to a painting of a sunburst.

“I don’t know,” frowned May. “Maybe it’s the weapon they spoke of.”

“Should we go down?” asked Noa.

“No,” said May. “It’s getting late, and we don’t want to do this in the dark. It will be completely void of light down there anyway. It would be nice if we at least had light up here to guide us back.”

“May, you’ve waited years for this,” said Mila empathetically. “We can suffer through a little darkness.”

“It’s okay,” she smiled. “I can wait another night. Tomorrow, I’ll get to enjoy whatever it is with my new friends. My love.” Thomas grinned at her, blushing.

“Alright, everyone, let’s set up camp,” said Bron. “Hiro and Marc, if you’ll gather wood for the fire. Ian, Fitch, and Frank set the tents up in a circle around the fire. We’ll tie the horses off to the tree, just in case we need them to get the hell out of here.”

Busying themselves at the camp, May stood just inside the tomb, staring at the images. She snapped several photographs, hoping that if for some horrible reason she was blocked out, she could review them more carefully.

She hoped this was Kahn’s tomb, but it could be anyone’s at this point. It could have been another leader, another king, who believed they were the great king. It was even possible it was a

Russian king or ruler with the borders being so close to one another. She touched the paintings, paintings that hadn't seen light in hundreds of years.

"What does Wǔqì mean?" asked Noah.

May jumped, startled by the interruption of her thoughts, and turned to stare at the big blonde. He reminded her of an ancient Viking, tall, blonde, blue-eyed, and fierce in his expression.

"Wh-where did you hear that?" asked May. Hiro frowned at his friend, stepping closer.

"It means weapon, brother," said Hiro.

"The child, she didn't know my word for it, but she says there is a weapon inside that we need to be careful of." He turned and walked away, leaving May standing with her mouth wide open.

"And they say I need to be better with my words," smirked Thomas.

"He can really hear them, can't he? The ghosts?" asked Mila. Bron nodded at her, watching as May backed out of the entrance to the tomb.

"He can, and so can Julia, Joseph's wife. She can hear them, see them, and speak to them. Noah can only see, hear, and speak to children, for some reason. He's seen a few adults, but they usually have a personal tie to him."

"That's unbelievable," whispered Mila.

"That's RP."

CHAPTER EIGHTEEN

1219

The thundering sound of the horses of a hundred thousand soldiers echoed across the steppe. Behind them, another thousand were escorting families. Twenty oxen pulled the great king's hut, his home, while they conquered the world.

Unlike any other army, their scouts could travel a hundred miles a day to gather the intelligence needed to win their battles. His most trusted men rode beside him.

"Great King, it may not be there when we arrive. Fighting the Persians will keep us busy enough without searching for this mysterious rock." He looked at his officer and just glared at him. The man obediently bowed his head.

"It is written that a once great king of Egypt cast a sword from this rock. It was so powerful even he could not contain its energy. If this will help me to conquer more worlds, then I will use it to provide for my people."

"But, Great King, how will we know when we find it?"

"I will know. I will know because Buddha and all the Gods of the world have sent it to earth for me, believing my vision is the one true vision. They have trusted me with this rock, and my spies tell me it's there. We will ride until we find this weapon, and when we do, we will create something that the world has never seen before."

As the dig began on the hill, Alec received word that the network gave the okay for Garvin to get on the next flight to China and then on to Mongolia. If they were right, they had about twenty-four hours before the asshole would descend on their location.

"We have to move this along, Dr. Roth," said Tailor. "Garvin is on his way, which gives us less than two days. If there is something here, we need to be sure that you're the one that finds it."

"We cannot rush this," he said, shaking his head. "If we try to dig too quickly, we could create a cave-in or cause damage to the structure. I'd rather see him find it than harm the site." Tailor and Alec nodded, realizing that Dr. Roth truly was interested in the historical value of the site, not the value of what was in the site.

He instructed the diggers to move more quickly but also with caution, moving thousands of pounds of dirt by the first day. Alec held up the LIDAR once again and smiled.

"Doc? Looks like you've only a few more feet to go." He pointed to the spikes on the screen, then transferred the images to the computer.

"Oh, my," he whispered. Tailor slapped Alec on the back and nodded toward the pile of dirt.

"Let's get to this, brother."

With Tailor and Alec digging, the pile increased ten-fold within just a few short hours. But they were losing daylight. Alec jammed the shovel into the earth, hitting something solid. He tapped it again and smiled, laying it by his side. Using his hands, he moved the earth aside, his hands running along the cold stone.

"That's it," whispered Dr. Roth. "You've found it."

"Then we keep going," said Tailor. "Set up the lights and keep digging. We don't have time to waste, and we need to see if this is the tomb or something else."

Ian and Marc stayed at the top of the stairs, ready to run for help should the cave collapse beneath the weight of the men and women inside, or just as terrifying, defend it should they need to do so.

May walked down the steps first, followed by Mila. The smooth stone stairs had not been stepped on in hundreds of years. The bright lights of the flashlights behind them illuminated the way. On the walls, all the way down, were scenes of great battles depicted in the pigments of the region. At the bottom of the stairs, there was an intricately carved coffin, gold handles and corners. There were depictions of war, children, and wildlife along its sides.

"Is this it?" whispered Thomas. He wasn't sure why he was whispering. He just felt as though he should.

"I think it is," nodded May, a tear falling down her cheek. "I can't believe it. He must have seen the sarcophaguses in Egypt. It's somewhat modeled after that style, except, of course, with Chinese and Mongol culture on the sides. It makes me wonder if he's mummified, but I don't want to lift the lid just yet."

"What do we do?" asked Mila.

"Hey," called Frank. "There's another box over here. It looks just like the casket, only smaller. It's just sitting in this recess in the wall."

"There's one here, too," said Parker in the other corner.

"Don't touch the casket," she said. "Sometimes they rigged these so that looters couldn't break into them, but more than that, it needs to be opened in a controlled environment." Walking toward the boxes against the wall, she ran her hands over them and smiled.

"What's in the boxes?" asked Bron.

"Well," she said, gently touching the lid of the first one. "I believe this contains gold and riches from his conquests."

She opened the lid, and everyone huddled closer, staring down into the small box. It was about two-feet wide, two-feet deep, and about three-feet high. Hundreds of gold coins with Kahn's head were gleaming back at them. Mixed with them were jewels, diamonds, emeralds, rubies, topaz, sapphires. There were several pieces of fabric already decaying due to the humidity and weather in the area. She didn't touch any of it, gently closing the lid.

Slowly walking to the other one, she frowned at the images of the sunburst, similar to that of the painting on the wall above them. Reaching into her pack, she put on rubber gloves and the safety goggles she'd brought with her as well as a mask.

"Stand back," she whispered.

"What? Fuck no," growled Thomas. "You're not opening that damn box by yourself." He put on his own gloves and mask and stepped forward. May smiled at him, nodding. Gently lifting the lid, she just stared at the contents.

"What is it?" asked Bron.

"There are five large, black rocks," said Thomas. "If I had to guess, they're from a meteor, but I can't be sure until I examine them in a lab. There are also five glass vials, but it doesn't look like there's anything in them. I should still be able to get residue from them."

"We need to gently carry this up, but I need something to wrap around these vials so that they won't bang together. I'm going to leave the box, but carry the rocks and vials out of here," said May. "Bron? Can you call the other site and tell Dr. Roth to get here right now? Also, call the Mongolian Ministry of Archaeology and get them here. We want Dr. Roth to get the credit for this with witnesses and cameras."

Bron raced back up the stone stairs and, as soon as he hit daylight, connected the satellite phone and told Alec and Tailor to get Dr. Roth to their location. He then made the call to the ministry. Just as he finished all the calls, Frank and Thomas were carefully bringing up the glass vials wrapped inside their quilted vests.

"Evie's on her way with the Osprey," said Bron. "Get it on that damn thing. Thomas? You and May need to be long gone before the Mongolian Ministry of Archaeology arrives. We don't want them to see you carrying that damn thing away, plus we want to ensure that Roth gets the credit for the find. It's time to give Garvin a taste of his own medicine."

"Dr. Roth, we have to go," said Tailor, standing above the small man who was digging carefully around the pillar.

"What? No! We can't leave this. It's a temple. This could be it." He looked at the men with a pain-stricken face.

"It's not," whispered Alec, leaning down. "We have to go now. Garvin is on his way here with cameras. Leave this for him. We've got the site."

"You have the site? Oh my God," he whispered.

"Let's go, sir."

Tailor practically carried the man to the Osprey, where Evie was waiting. Less than twenty minutes later, they were landing near the lake. Dr. Roth ran as fast as his old, withered legs could carry him.

"It's him," smiled May. "It's him, Dr. Roth." She hugged him gently, his frail old body breathing heavily from the rush of adrenaline and excitement.

"May. May, this is your find," he said.

"No, I don't need this find," she said, grabbing Thomas's hand. "I found something worth a lot more than this. Besides, Garvin is going to be very angry. The ministry is on its way here. You handle the site with Alec and Tailor. We'll handle the other item we found."

"You found it?" he asked.

"Maybe," she said, shrugging. "I promise you, it's the only thing we took, and if it turns out to be nothing, we'll find a way to get it back to you."

"We have to get out of here before the Mongolian government shows up, May," said Thomas.

"Go," said Mila. "You two go with the contents of the box, and we'll stay here. Get it somewhere safe, and we'll see you at home." May turned to her new friend, hugging her tightly.

"Thank you, Mila. Thank you for giving me the chance to prove that I can do it." Mila kissed her friend's cheek, waving as the helicopter lifted off with Thomas and May.

"Dr. Roth, I'm Bron Jones. Why don't you let me show you what we've found?" Bron smiled at the older man as he nodded, nervously walking toward the cave. Bron and Frank led him down to the burial tomb, and the old man just stood there, shaking his head with tears in his eyes.

"Are you alright, sir?" asked Frank.

"Young man, when you've waited a lifetime to prove that your work is worth something, that it has meaning, this is a moment when it's okay to cry. It's definitely Kahn. The scenes depicted are of his battles across the world. Russia, Poland, India, they're all there. The children represent those he saved, spawned, and adopted. The animals represent those he saw in his travels. Animals he hoped to bring home, here to Mongolia for all to see.

"And this," he said, pointing to a figure of a woman with long, flowing hair, "this is no doubt the only woman he ever truly loved. We don't know her name, but she was obviously important to him."

"Do you open the casket?" asked Frank.

"Eventually, but we'll get the government involved in that. They'll want their own archaeologists involved in this, and rightfully so. What about Garvin? Can you keep him away?" asked Dr. Roth.

"We will definitely keep him away," smirked Bron.

CHAPTER NINETEEN

"What is this? Why is this site already being excavated?" asked Garvin of the workers sitting on the side of the hill. They quickly explained that another man had started the dig and then suddenly left.

Garvin stepped forward, cameras following his every move. He touched the stone of the temple, then turned toward the camera.

"Turn it off," he growled. "This isn't it. He wouldn't have left if it was it."

"Dr. Garvin? We're getting reports of a find north of here. The Mongolian government is already there."

"No," he said, shaking his head, "no, this can't be happening."

Garvin and his team loaded up into the hired helicopter and took off toward the other location. Dozens of people swarmed the area, government and military officials alike. He practically leaped from the helicopter, running toward the roped-off area.

"I'm sorry, sir, only dig team members can access this site," said Ian, pushing back on the man. He recognized him immediately when he came running toward them, knowing what he was going to try and do.

"Do you know who I am? I own this site," he said with a pompous attitude.

"No, you fucking don't," growled Ian, pushing back on his chest. "You own nothing. Not this site, not this dig, not these findings. Dr. Donald Roth owns this dig. Him and the people of Mongolia."

"Roth?" he scoffed, then began laughing. "If Roth is here, it's probably nothing."

"It is not nothing," growled Noah from behind Garvin. Garvin turned, staring up at the behemoth behind him. He swallowed, taking a step back. Ian looked at the cameraman and rolled his fingers in a circular motion, telling him to get this on camera. Ian wanted the world to see the fear in the man's eyes and that he wasn't as big and tough as he pretended to be. "This is the tomb of Genghis Kahn."

"No," said Garvin, shaking his head. "No, this is my find!"

"Dude, you didn't hear my friend," smirked Tailor, stepping closer. "You don't belong here. You don't touch anything. You don't own anything, and you damn sure didn't find anything. I was here when Dr. Roth made the discovery. It's his. Funded by a very generous benefactor."

"Is this man creating a disturbance?" asked the officer of the Mongolian Armed Forces.

"Mr. Garvin..."

"Dr. Garvin!" he yelled.

"My apologies," smirked Frank. "Dr. Garvin has nothing to do with this dig. However, he is attempting to break into it and take credit for the dig himself."

"It's mine!"

"Do you have proof of that?" asked the officer. "I will need to see your papers that allowed you to dig at this site. I have seen those from Dr. Roth."

"I-I don't have that with me," he said, puffing out his chest.

"Dr. Garvin is notorious for stealing the credit of major archaeological finds," said Tailor. "He somehow believes his status with network television allows him the right to do such things."

"That is a crime in my country," said the officer. "It would be punishable by death."

Garvin shook his head, paling at that statement. He backed up, then ran toward his helicopter, and disappeared. Frank, Alec, and Tailor turned toward the man in uniform.

"Nice job, Hiro," smirked Frank. "Where the fuck did you get the uniform?"

"Oh, I paid a guard five hundred U.S. dollars to let me borrow it. I should probably get it back to him. He's naked in that truck over there." The men laughed, shaking their heads as Hiro took off toward the truck.

It was a whirlwind of activity as reporters descended on the dig site. Dr. Donald Roth was an international celebrity. The tomb of Kahn would be guarded and undisturbed, but it at least was discovered, and he would get the credit.

Later that evening, as the media left the location, leaving only permanent military guards and the RP men, Dr. Roth walked toward the huge fire.

"Quite a day for you, Dr. Roth," smiled Bron.

"Please, just Donald. I have no words for all of you, none. This is a dream come true. I don't understand why Dr. Wong would give this discovery to me, but I am grateful for it."

"You're going to be famous," smiled Fitch. "Are you going to do an adventure show like Garvin?" Roth laughed, shaking his head.

"I was once told that I have a face made for radio," he smiled. The men all laughed, shaking their heads. "I think I'll leave the celebrity digging to someone like Garvin. It suits his ego. Do we have any word from May?"

"They're on their way back to the RP compound. Thomas and the others will examine the contents of the box, and we'll know something then. Right now, just enjoy this, Donald. We'll be heading out tomorrow, but the Mongolian military is going to remain, and of course, you'll need a few months to catalog everything that was in that tomb."

"You know, you search your whole life to find something that hasn't been touched or seen by a human in hundreds, hopefully, thousands of years. I first made the decision to enter this field when as a young man, I read about Pompeii. Then I started studying the great Pyramids, the valley of the kings, Machu Pichu. I was hooked on everything old and dead," he laughed. "Thanks to all of you, twenty years from now, a young man will read in a book about Dr. Donald Roth, archaeologist and adventurer, who discovered the lost burial site of Genghis Kahn."

The men were silent as they watched tears fall down Roth's face. Mila stood, walked around the fire, and sat next to him.

"We have another surprise for you, Dr. Roth," said Mila. "We spoke to the Mongolian government, and you've been given exclusive dig access to the other site as well. It's not Kahn, but it's a major find, and you should get credit for that as well. A private organization will be funding the dig for you and paying for security. Garvin won't bother you again."

"Oh, my," he whispered. "Thank you. Thank you, all." He walked back to his tent as the people around the fire watched him.

"What do you think is in the other site?" Bron asked Mila.

"I was asking May that very question," she said. "She thinks it could be a temple that pre-dates Kahn. It might have been too difficult to take down, so he simply covered it, or Kahn was much smarter than anyone believes. He may have actually understood the importance of not destroying it. From the readings you all sent, she said it appears to be completely intact. It might be a bigger find than this."

"Unbelievable," smirked Alec. "You know, we'd go on all those adventures around Belle Fleur and find arrowheads and cannonballs and shit and never think anything of it. Adele was always juiced by it, but the rest of us didn't pay much attention to it."

"When we found that surprise in the Sugar Lodge, I suppose that gave me an appreciation for history and what it might have to offer," said Frank.

"There is still one thing," said Mila. "We don't know who killed Lora and Mike. I need to know that. I need to solve it, and I don't have much time left on my leave."

"Yea, we need to solve it," said Bron, squeezing her hand. Parker looked at the group and nodded.

"We won't solve it tonight. Our ride arrives at 0800. Get some sleep."

CHAPTER TWENTY

It would be three days later before everyone was able to meet once again about what was in the tomb and the murders. It took almost twenty-four hours to get home and another twenty to catch up on their sleep, and another ten to sift through the information they'd collected along the way.

Mila was getting incredibly nervous, mostly because her leave time was up. She'd begged for one more day, and it was granted, but that was the last of it. If she didn't report for duty the next day, she could be fired.

"My initial thoughts were correct," said Thomas. He lifted the black rocks in his hand. "The rocks were from a meteor, but not one that hit Mongolia or China. I think this hit somewhere in the Middle East, perhaps Persia or Egypt, based on the elements that were attached to it. I'm not sure how Kahn knew its value, but it's unlike any other meteor I've ever seen or studied."

"How so?" asked Bron.

"Most meteors are made of silicon and oxygen and usually heavier metals like nickel and iron. The nickel and iron make them incredibly dense and massive. Those that are more stone-like are lighter and usually don't make it to earth. They either break up or move in another direction. This meteor contained all of those things, but also a very unusual element I haven't seen before.

"Initially, I thought it was plutonium, but that seemed impossible. It doesn't test as the same density and isn't emitting radioactivity. On closer examination, it's something as yet undiscovered."

"Is that what would make it a weapon?" asked Bron.

"It's unlikely," said Thomas, reaching for the glass vials. "These are what would make it a weapon. The liquid is long gone, but there are traces of nitroglycerin."

"Nitro?" frowned Miller in the back row. "That's impossible. It wasn't discovered until the mid-1800s."

"That's what makes this extraordinary," smiled Thomas. "It appears that Kahn and his chemists were able to formulate it long before anyone else. You have to remember that the Chinese were using gunpowder for explosives long before it was being placed in a rifle or a bullet. If you combined nitro with a ground-up version of this rock, it could create an unbelievable explosion. My guess is that they found it quite by accident.

"Kahn was ruthless, some say a murderer, but he obviously knew what this weapon would do to mankind. To my knowledge, this has never been found before in an archaeological dig. It's truly remarkable, and it's unfortunate we cannot tell anyone," said Thomas.

"He's right," said May. "It's too risky. However, it does raise questions as to how anyone knew about this being in the tomb. The maps, notes, documents, etcetera, found on Lora and Mike don't tell us how they got the information, other than we think they took it from files and documents off the base."

"Why would the Marine Corps tell their people they believed it was a new weapons system? I mean, they had to have known where this was," said Bron.

"Maybe not," said Mila, shaking her head. "Maybe they heard the same rumors as everyone else and thought it was a weapons factory. Either way, we need to find out how Lora and Mike got that information and were then able to leave us detailed clues on how to get there."

"We may not ever know, Mila," said Bron. "We need to be prepared for that."

Mila stood, shaking her head as she paced back and forth around the room. The men stared at her, uncertain as to why she was so tied to this. Yes, Lora was her roommate, and yes, someone had murdered her. But this seemed more personal to Mila than it should.

The door to the auditorium opened, and Mila stared at the man she'd met a few days ago, Sly. He stared back at her, then looked down at his tablet and back up at her.

"Sly? What's up, brother?" asked Luke.

"Maybe Mila would like to tell you that information," he said, staring at the woman. Bron turned, looking at Mila. She swallowed, tears coming to her eyes as she shook her head.

"I knew someone would find out. It doesn't matter anymore. Nothing matters anymore," she said.

"What doesn't matter anymore?" asked Bron, folding his big arms across his chest. "Enlighten us."

"Mike Hartfeld was my adopted brother, Pete. My parents changed his name when they took him to that boarding school in England. That's why I couldn't find him. They didn't want me to find him," she said, staring at the room. She looked at Bron, shaking her head. "You thought it was Lora that stalked me and intentionally ran into me. It was the other way around. She was already dating Pete, I mean, Mike, and I wanted to get close to him, to see how he was doing.

"He didn't recognize me at first. It's been more than twenty years since we'd seen one another. Finally, he confronted me. He knew I was CID and begged me not to tell them about the name change and his learning challenges. You made the comment that you were shocked he passed his tests for MARSOC. That's because of his disabilities, and he didn't want the military to know. He'd become a master at covering them up. The boarding school discovered that he was on the autism spectrum, but with the right tools and teaching, he was highly capable.

"I was glad that he and Lora were happy. I was truthful about not knowing what they were doing in China. I had no clue. When I got word that they were killed, I felt as though my whole world tumbled around me. He was all I had left. The only link to an otherwise rotten childhood.

"Look, I don't know why they were trying to find this weapon, or even if that's what they were actually doing, but I know that neither Mike or Lora would have used this to start a war or to sell it."

"People have done it before," frowned Bron. He took a step forward, his gaze boring into her. "You lied to us."

"I didn't lie about anything," she said, shaking her head. "It didn't matter that Mike was my adopted brother. Lora was your ex-wife. Why would any of that matter?"

"You would have told us if you didn't really think it mattered," said Cam, staring at the woman. She started to speak, then closed her mouth. "CID knows you're here, and they want to know why."

"Wh-what?" she gasped.

"They called here this morning. They said you were seen by someone at the airport with our team. Apparently, you're two days late returning from leave." Cam looked at Bron, then at Luke and Eric. "You can stay if you want, Mila, but no more lies. Even by omission. We don't operate that way."

"I'm not two days late. I asked for an extra day, and it was given. I need to call them," she said, turning to face Bron. She couldn't tell what the expression was on his face, but it wasn't a happy one. He seemed pissed off, but there was something else there as well. "I-I'd like to stay."

Leaving the room to see if she still had a job, Bron turned to the others.

"I didn't know."

"Bron, brother, we never thought you did," said Luke. "In the grand scheme of things, it wasn't all that important, other than she needed to be upfront with us."

"What do we know about Garvin and his history?" asked Bron thoughtfully. "I mean, if he's willing to steal information to take credit for a site dig, how far would he go to get the information to find one? More importantly, what the fuck were Lora and Mike doing stealing this information?"

"He's never been arrested for anything," said Ace, "but he has been sued a number of times. In fact, almost every find he was credited with came with controversy. He's a total tool."

"Let's start with him," said Cam. "We'll all take a look at the records from the murder scene again and then meet up in the morning. Bron? Talk to her, brother. She's worth it."

CHAPTER TWENTY-ONE

Mila waited for the ranting of her supervisor to stop so that she could get a word in edgewise. The man was relentless, berating her and telling her she was a disgrace to CID. He'd made his opinions clear from the moment she stepped foot into his office. He didn't want women in his division, and he'd do anything to drive them out. He'd made her life miserable, and this was just putting the nail in the coffin.

"Look, Agent Lambton, I get that your roommate was murdered, but that was weeks ago. I mean, how much damn time do you need to get over this?" Mila could only silently shake her head at the phone. "You're ruining your career."

"Consider me resigned," she said quietly.

"What did you just say?" he barked.

"I said, consider me resigned. I'm done. That's what you've wanted all along anyway. I'll have someone clear out my desk and send my things, but I won't be back, sir."

"You have to come back and sign out. You'll need to go through the official process of resignation, Agent Lambton. This is the United States government, in case you've forgotten."

"How could I forget, sir? You've reminded me of it every damn day of my employment. You take great delight in telling me how incompetent I am, how women don't make great CID agents, how I should be in another field. You've enjoyed those moments more than a man should, and you can be damn sure on my exit I will tell everyone that!" She hit end, spinning around and throwing the phone toward the door.

Instead of the loud crash she expected, Bron was standing in the doorway, her phone in his hand.

“Nice arm,” he smirked. It immediately started ringing again, and he answered it. “She’s busy. Call back later.” He turned the phone off and slid it across the table.

“Why are you here? To tell me you hate me? To tell me I need to leave? To tell me...”

“Shut up,” he said, moving toward her. “Just shut up for five minutes. I’m here to tell you that I don’t like that you withheld that information from us, but you were right. It didn’t have any impact on any of this. However, we don’t leave anything out around here. We don’t lie about details, and we don’t hold things back from one another. If you and I are going to be married, we’ll need to learn to...”

“Wh-what? Married?” she whispered.

“I asked you not to interrupt me,” he smiled. “If we’re going to be married, we need to know that we can tell one another anything and everything. For instance, I can tell you that I hate broccoli, but I love spinach. I don’t like ice cream, but I love cake.”

“Y-you want to marry me?”

“Did you get hit on the head in that tomb? Yes, I want to marry you, Mila. You’re everything I’ve ever wanted in a woman, and your sexual appetite matches mine perfectly. We don’t have to do it today or tomorrow, but we will get married...”

“Yes.”

“You’re just intent on interrupting me, aren’t you?” he said, shaking his head. “That might call for a spanking.”

“Yes,” she said again with a hiccup as tears streamed down her face. “Yes to it all.” Leaping into his arms, he held her tightly, kissing her neck, inhaling her perfume.

“Don’t ever lie to me again, baby.”

"I promise. I swear to God! I thought I lost you," she cried. "I thought I'd have to leave here and never be able to see you again."

"You're not quite that lucky," he smirked. "You're going to be seeing me for a very, very long time. I love you, Mila. I've loved you since the moment you started annoying me." She laughed, kissing him again, still wrapped around his body.

"What do we do about Lora and Mike?"

"We're working on that. For now, let's try to figure out how all of this is fitting together. I want to understand how they knew about the box of materials that were on the base and how Garvin would have found it as well."

"Do we have time?" she asked, running her tongue from his ear to neck, then to his lips.

"Fucking right we do," he growled. He dropped her feet to the floor, bending her over the sofa. Lowering her shorts to the floor, he drove his big fingers in and out, readying her for his hardening cock.

"Oh, Bron," she moaned, "yea, baby, yea. More."

He removed his fingers and slammed his cock in her sweet pussy, driving hard against her body. With his fingers still wet, he swirled around her tight hole and thrust one in, then two.

"God! Bron, yes!"

"That's it," he growled, bending over her back. "Fucking cum for me. You're mine, Mila. Mine!"

She screamed so loud Bron was certain that someone would be pounding on the door any second now. When he pulled out of her, he saw the creamy drip of his body and realized something. He hadn't used a condom at all. In fact, he didn't remember using a condom once with her.

"Baby, I'm sorry, but I haven't been using a condom at all."

"It's okay," she said, shaking her head. "I'm on the patch, and I'm clean. I haven't been with anyone in over a year." He nodded, kissing her as he tucked his dick back in his pants.

"Same. We get tested here, and I'm clean. I haven't been with anyone in about six months, and it was nothing serious."

"What do you mean?" she asked, frowning at him.

"Well, uh, total honesty?" Mila nodded, taking a seat at the bar. "Women tend to hang around bars that military guys go to, you know that. They're looking for permanent, but most of the guys are looking to get laid. Sorry, I don't mean to be crass. I was always honest with women, Mila. I told them it was one time and one time only. I didn't bring them home with me. If they wanted sex, it was at their place or a hotel."

"So, you've done a lot of one-night stands?" she asked.

"I don't consider them that," he said, shaking his head. "I think of a one-night stand as a guy promising the girl something and then ditching her. I made sure they understood. If they made any indication they wanted more, I left. Simple as that."

"But what if you left a woman you were supposed to be with?"

"Not possible," he said, stepping closer to kiss her nose. "The woman I'm supposed to be with is standing right in front of me. I don't know if it's some kind of magic here, but it happens a lot. Or, maybe, Lora planned all this out. I don't know." He shook his head, kissing her once again.

"She showed me your picture," she said, staring up at him. "For some reason, she still had a picture of the two of you on your wedding day. I have to say, the uniform was freaking sexy."

Bron laughed, shaking his head.

"She said it wasn't your fault. It was hers, and if she could do it all over again, she would have said 'no.' I remember looking at that photo before I came out here to find you and thinking, how could anyone ever leave a man that looked like you. It wasn't just the way you looked. It was the expression in your eyes. It's this steely, hard gaze that tells people to back up."

"That's what the Marine Corps does to you," he grinned.

"Maybe. I do love you, Bron. I don't know when it happened, but beyond the sex being off the charts amazing, I love the man that you are, the teammate."

"Good," he said, smiling down at her. "Let's go grab some lunch and see if we figure out what the fuck is going on."

CHAPTER TWENTY-TWO

"How did they know where to find it? And more importantly, how was my information wrong?" asked Garvin.

"We're not sure," said the man seated across from him. "Everything you were given came directly from their belongings in the hotel room. We copied everything before the cops got to it. The maps, the books, the notes, all of it."

"Well, that's lovely, except now I'm knee-deep in shit-water," he spat. "The Koreans and Russians both bid on what was in that burial site, and now I have nothing to show them, nothing to give them. Do you understand what this will do to my reputation?"

The other man just stared at him, not really giving a shit what it did to his reputation. He wanted the money that was owed to him. He'd done everything the man asked, including betraying his country.

"Look, I was the one that overheard the commander telling the generals about the site. I was the one that told you about the potential for a weapon and that they believed they knew where it was located. I did all of that. The least you could do is be grateful. There will be other digs, Garvin."

"That was my dig," he sneered. "Fucking loser Roth. That old man wouldn't know a good dig if he fell into the hole. Can we kill him?"

The man seated across from him just shook his head. That was his response to everything that didn't go his way. Kill whoever was blocking him. The real world didn't work that way.

"No, you can't kill him. The site is guarded by the Mongolian military as well as top-notch private security. Besides, it wouldn't matter. It's his find now, and according to everyone I've spoken to, there are no signs of a weapon being hidden in the tomb."

"I want that site!" he yelled.

He'd had enough. Standing, he tossed a five-dollar bill on the table to pay for his coffee. He grabbed his jacket and looked down at the little pissant movie star.

"A little advice, Garvin. Stop throwing fucking temper tantrums and move on. This one is not yours. Find another one. Find Atlantis. Find Alexander the Great. Fuck, I don't care, find the Easter bunny. Just give this one up. You won't win."

He turned, leaving the little man to seethe under his breath. Garvin had been a pain in his ass since day one. He never intended on helping him, but he was in debt up to his eyeballs, and he paid well. Going from SEAL to grave robber wasn't exactly what he'd intended to do. Now, he needed to make things right.

Dialing the number, he waited until the voice answered.

"Fucking Tim Pearson," growled Frank. "What's up, brother?"

"Frank, I fucked up, brother. We need to talk."

"Okay, I've got time now."

"No. I need to talk face-to-face. You're not going to like it, but I'm going to ask that you hear me out and then let me go. I won't fucking bother you again, I promise."

"What the hell, Tim. What's going on?"

"Please, Frank. I'll come to you."

"Okay. Café 22, south of New Orleans. When can I expect you?" asked Frank.

"I'll be there on the next flight. I'll meet you for dinner. And Frank, bring Luke and Cam and tell them I'm sorry."

"Hey, Tim, whatever it is, we can figure it out, brother. It's what we fucking do, you know that."

"Not this time, Frank."

CHAPTER TWENTY-THREE

"What do you think this is about?" asked Cam.

"I don't know, man. All I know is he sounded distraught. When I spoke to him in San Diego, he said Catherine was pushing him to retire and go to work for her father. Maybe he did that, and something happened," said Frank with a shrug.

Just as he finished speaking, they spotted Tim Pearson walking into the café. He looked around, and his eyes landed on Frank, Cam, and Luke. Giving a head nod, he headed to the booth, shaking their hands.

"It's good to see you, brother," smiled Cam. Tim frowned, shaking his head.

"Hey, man, what's up?" asked Luke. "It's all good. We'll help if we can."

"That's just it. You can't."

"Last time I saw you, Tim, you were thinking about coming to work for us. Did you go to work for your father-in-law?"

"No, worse. Catherine, she's always been a handful. Always spending more money than I could make and running to her daddy for help. This last time, he gave an ultimatum, either I find a job making enough money to give his baby girl the life she deserved, or they were going to file for divorce with the best attorneys in the state, and I'd lose everything. My pension, all of it."

"We can help, Tim," said Luke. The other man held up a hand, shaking his head again.

"It's so fucked-up. She threw a fit one night at dinner, and the guy at the table next to us started talking to me while she was crying in the bathroom. He said he'd give me five hundred thousand for one job. One fucking job."

"Brother, you know the old saying, if it sounds too good to be true?" smirked Cam.

"Yea, I know. Anyway, he said there was a Marine at Pendleton that had something he wanted. Something he needed." The table shifted. Frank, Cam, and Luke stiffened, staring at Tim. "All I had to do was get the information from him. Mike Hartfeld wasn't exactly the brightest bulb in the box, but he was a good Marine. I convinced him to help me get the information that was being discussed at a meeting at Pendleton.

"He had no fucking clue, man. He was dating this woman, and I think when he brought the information home, she figured it out. They were supposed to meet us at a location in China, but they didn't show. The man I'm working for, he found them in San Francisco. He killed them, man. I might as well have pulled the trigger myself, although he chose poison.

"This guy is a fucking dick all the way. He's so full of himself it's not even funny. The brass thought it was a weapons factory or some shit, but it was an ancient tomb that supposedly had some sort of weapon in it. Something happened, and the information was wrong. The location was wrong, everything. Somebody else found it, got the credit for it, and now he's on the warpath.

"He took bids from the Russians and the Koreans, and now he can't deliver. It's all so fucked-up, I can't even begin to tell you."

The table was deathly silent for several long minutes as each man sipped his coffee. Luke finally looked up and spoke.

"This man wouldn't happen to be Rock Garvin?" Tim frowned. His eyes went wide, but then he nodded at him.

"How did you know that?"

"Has he taken money from anyone for the find yet?" asked Cam.

"Only from the network, I think. He promised them the tomb was a sure thing, and they'd get the exclusive on the find. They gave him about four million upfront, and believe me, he spends it as fast as he gets it. Women, cars, clothes, plastic surgery, tattoos, everything. Bastard should have married Catherine. They'd make a great pair."

"Did he pay you?" asked Cam.

"He handed me a check this morning," said Tim, pulling it from his pocket and sliding it across the table. "I couldn't cash it. I just couldn't do it. I haven't taken any other payment from him."

"Who killed Mike and the woman?" asked Frank.

"I didn't tell you there was a woman," he said cautiously. The others just stared at him, and he knew his ass was cooked. "One of Garvin's goons. He has this guy that will kill dig workers, anyone he wants for a few hundred bucks. He's nothing, really, which is why he poisons most people. He doesn't have to face them or fight them. He wouldn't have been able to take Mike in a fair fight, so he poisoned their food delivery."

"So, did you leave the SEALs?" asked Frank.

"Yea. I retired a month ago and went to work for this guy, but I can't do it, brother. I just can't. Catherine's gonna take everything I own, but I don't give a shit."

"Did you ever get a DNA test on the kid?" asked Frank.

"No," he said quietly.

"I don't agree with what you did, Tim, but I understand the reasons why you did it. If you want, we can help you figure your marital situation out, get the DNA test. Our attorneys can help you with that. Share whatever you can about Garvin, and we'll make sure you're left out of that situation."

"He's not going to give up. He's pissed about not getting this dig. He hates Roth and some other archaeologist named Wong."

"Tim, our team is the one that took Roth to that site. We've got a team of men guarding him along with the military. They won't get to him. As for Wong," grinned Cam, "she's on the compound with one of our men."

"Fuck, seriously?" smirked Tim.

"Will you help us?" asked Luke.

"Fuck, you know I will. I didn't know what the hell to do. I came to the only people I thought might stop this asshole. I had no idea you guys were already involved."

"What's the man's name that killed Mike and Lora?" asked Frank.

"He goes by the name Critter Pine. That describes him, too. He's like a cockroach, always showing up even after you think he's dead. I think his real name is Bert or something stupid."

"Okay, let's go," said Frank.

"Wait, where are we going?"

"Beyond those gates over there is our compound. This café is owned and operated by our family. Everything you see for miles belongs to RP. We're gonna help you, Tim, but then you're going to do some things for us."

"Anything," he said, nodding. "I know I don't deserve your help, but I do appreciate anything you can do for me."

"You put them in harm's way," whispered Mila. "Mike didn't deserve that, neither did Lora. I don't agree with what he did, but he tried to correct it once he knew what it was."

"I know," he said, shaking his head. "I know, and I'm so fucking sorry for that. I never thought Garvin would have them killed."

"But he did," cried Mila. "He killed my brother. The only family I have. You're a SEAL. You're supposed to protect people."

"Mila, honey, maybe you need to step out of the room," said Bron. She shook her head.

"No, I'm staying. I know you didn't mean for them to be murdered, but you had to have known that they weren't going to win against Garvin. From what we know, he's just an evil, narcissistic asshole."

"He is that," frowned Tim.

"Hey, Tim?" called Code from his spot behind his computer. "We have some information you might be interested in. The child, Alexis?"

"Yes," he said quietly, swallowing, waiting for the next statement.

"She had a small lump removed from her back about six months ago. From that tissue analysis and the blood work done, we were able to compare it to yours. Brother, there's no way the child is yours." Tim swallowed, tears in his eyes as he nodded. "Tim, I'm sorry, man. Her DNA is her mother's, but also a male of primarily African and Brazilian descent."

"I knew. Somewhere inside me, I knew. Dunc and the other guys kept telling me, but I wouldn't believe them." Mila watched as the man's heart cracked in two, and she couldn't help but feel sorry for him. "She's the cutest fucking kid, and now I'll never see her again."

"I'm sorry," said Mila. "Really, I'm very sorry about that."

"Thanks."

"Where will Garvin go next?" asked Luke.

"He's still got a hard-on for the site in Mongolia," said Tim. "My guess is he's going to try and kill Roth, but if you've got men on him, that won't happen. He's crazy enough that he actually might try to blow the tomb."

"No!" yelled May. Tim looked up at the tiny woman standing next to a very large, overprotective man. He wore wire-rimmed glasses, but that was where his nerdiness ended. He reminded Tim of Dunc, long, tall, lean muscles that rippled when he breathed. "He can't blow that site. He just can't!"

"I'm sorry, ma'am, but he's just that kind of crazy," said Tim. "He would do anything to prove that he's the superior person in the field."

"Tim, this is May Wong."

"Dr. Wong," he said, shaking his head. "I'm sure you're not surprised to know that he hates you as much as he does Dr. Roth."

"I'm not surprised, nor do I care. He stole credit for my dig a long time ago, and he's done the same thing to almost every archaeologist in the world. His ego is the only thing bigger than the findings of everyone other than him."

"His ego," repeated Tim.

"That's right, he's got an ego the size of a whale. It's not about the dig or the find that's important to him. It's about the celebrity."

"Yes, I know, but maybe that's where we pull him out. Some crazy big award that he's won, or a dig that they want him to work. Something that will make him leave the site in Mongolia alone and come right to all of you."

"That's not enough," said Mila. "I want him to admit to ordering the kill on Mike and Lora. And if I were really wishing on the stars, I want him to admit to stealing the credit for the dig from May and the one for Dr. Roth."

"You don't want much, do you, baby?" smiled Bron.

"No, I don't think I do. I just want this asshole behind bars or dead, whichever is more convenient."

CHAPTER TWENTY-FOUR

1227 A.D.

"We cannot use this," said the great Kahn. "Should it be exposed to the world, there will be no world left."

"But my great leader, we could destroy entire cities with this," said his lead weapons master.

"Yes, I understand, but we will not. If I were to destroy all the cities and all the people in those cities, who would be left to become my loyal followers? Who? No. Your wisdom is not your own. Keep it in the box with the vials. When I am dead, bury it with me. That is my order. That is my wish."

"You will live long," said his vassal.

"I am dying. I know that I will not last long. I have conquered. I have fought. I have done everything to make the Mongols the greatest people in all of civilization. It is up to you to carry this work forward. But you must do it without me. Conquering the world on horseback is easy. Stepping off the horse and governing, that is hard."

His eyes closed, and they gathered around him, watching his breathing, raspy and harsh. Wives, children, and concubines lined up to say their goodbyes one last time for the great ruler. All around him, his soldiers stood guard. The best carpenters in the world carved the intricate designs on the box that would carry him home once again to his beloved land.

He'd ordered that it be simple. He wanted to be buried where no one would find him, no one would disturb him, and they were going to fulfill his wish.

When his last breath left his body, they hurriedly placed him in the coffin, and his troops marched, killing everyone in their path to ensure that no one knew the great Kahn was dead or where he was buried.

By the time they arrived, the tomb was ready, gleaming with torchlight as they carried him down the stairs. They left an offering for him of gold and jewels, silks, and tapestries. In the other box, they placed the strange rocks and the glass vials. On the outside of the box, the sunburst looked identical to what they'd witnessed just months before in the far-off desert. The sand and rock-strewn so far into the sky it darkened the earth below.

Now, it would be hidden for all time, and the great Kahn would finally be at rest.

"An action committed in anger is an action doomed to fail."

Genghis Kahn

CHAPTER TWENTY-FIVE

"Is this Dr. Rock Garvin?" asked the deep baritone voice. It sounded important. It commanded respect, and he straightened a bit, wondering if it were someone from the network.

"This is he," he answered crisply.

"Dr. Garvin, my name is Peter Webster. I'm with the International Explorers and Archaeologists Society, and I'm calling to notify you that you've been selected to receive our lifetime achievement award."

"I have?" he said, smiling into the phone. "Well, of course, that's not surprising considering my body of work. I'm honored. But you must understand, my time is extremely valuable, and I may not be available for the award."

"Dr. Garvin, we will be flying you via private jet to San Francisco, where you'll be receiving the award in the famous Japanese Gardens by lantern light. Part of the award is that you'll receive a ten-million-dollar prize to continue your explorations."

Garvin sucked in a deep breath and smiled. Take that old man Roth and that scrawny bitch, May. Famous, awards, and accolades, and the cash I'm so deserving.

"Well, that does change things a bit. It will take me a day or two to get back to San Francisco. I'm currently out of the country in Asia. I don't know if you've heard about the discovery on Genghis Kahn's tomb, but I was there, supporting the good Dr. Roth."

"No," said the voice on the other end of the line, "I hadn't heard that."

"Yes, well, part of being an exceptional explorer is knowing when to let other, lesser-known archaeologists have their day in the sun. Dr. Roth, sadly, is at the end of his time, where I'm at the beginning of mine."

"I understand."

"I'll look forward to receiving the arrangements for my flight and accommodations," he quipped. "I assume my airfare will be first-class."

"It's a private plane, Dr. Garvin. You'll have the whole thing to yourself. Where should we pick you up from?"

"My home in Las Vegas. I'll text you everything you need." He ended the call and stared at the man he called Critter. "After I'm gone for twenty-four hours, find a way to kill Dr. Roth. I'll be taking over this dig site one way or another."

"No problem," grinned the man. "Just send the money to the usual place."

Garvin sneered at him. He needed him, but that didn't mean he had to like him. Still sitting in the hotel in Beijing, he'd been weighing his options, wondering how he could get back out to the site and claim it as his own. The network was demanding their advance back, and he wasn't about to give it to them.

"Well, perhaps we'll win all the way around," he said, grinning at himself in the mirror. He straightened his hair, spritzing five too many pumps of cologne on his body. "Time for some local flavor, and I don't mean food."

"He bought it, hook, line, and sinker," said Miller. "And might I say what a fucking pompous asshole that guy is. May? How in the hell did you ever think he was worthy of you?"

"I'm not sure," she laughed, "but thank you for reminding me that I was right. I wouldn't put it past him to still send someone to hurt Dr. Roth."

"Don't you worry about that, honey. We've got a few boys sitting there, just waiting for the opportunity to take him out," smiled Luke.

"I feel like I should be doing something," said Mila. "I'm usually in on the investigations and arrests. I want to see this man taken down and make him accountable for the deaths of Lora and Mike."

"You can't see him, baby, but you will hear it. We'll all be wired, and when Tim approaches him, you'll hear everything he has to say. We're going to make sure this is iron-clad."

"What about this awards show? He's going to know when he arrives that something is wrong," said May.

"RP has connections everywhere," smiled Hiro. "I have friends with the National Parks Service as well as the San Francisco police department. Right now, tables and chairs are being set up in the gardens, along with a stage. Three nights from now, more than forty couples from here at RP will be dressed in their finest, waiting for the good doctor to show his face. Once Tim is able to get the information we need recorded, we'll take him down."

"Wow, well, I guess you all have everything together. What should I do?" asked Mila. Bron smiled down at her.

"Well, you could be talking to Mama Irene about a wedding," he grinned. Mila felt herself blush as all eyes turned toward her.

"I-I guess I could be doing that, couldn't I?" Thomas grinned at his friend, Bron, then turned to May.

"I've heard that double weddings are pretty special and one of the many things that Mama Irene does well," said Thomas. May stared up at him, her eyes wide, filled with tears. "I love you, May Wong. I'm not very good at saying it or showing it. I'm awkward, sometimes so focused on my work I'm drowning in it, but I know that I was sent here for this very reason. To be with you."

"You want to marry me?" she whispered. Bron laughed, shaking his head.

"Why do all of you say that? If we ask you to marry us, believe me, we're sincere." Mila smiled at her friend, nodding.

"Yes. I will marry you, Thomas Bradshaw, because you're the kindest, sweetest, smartest man I know, and you've got a killer body." The men in the room chuckled. "One thing. You're not going to post guards outside my lecture hall at the university, are you?"

"Well..." The doors flew open, and Mama Irene entered with Erin, Grace, and Faith, smiling at the two women.

"We heard wind of a double weddin'," smiled Irene, rubbing her hands together like a mad scientist.

"How the fuck does she do that?" frowned Fitch. CC leaned toward him and whispered.

"Don't ask, brother, don't ask. You're going to find that Mama Irene is able to do all sorts of things that are unexplainable. Drives her kids crazy."

"Yes, ma'am, I guess there will be a double wedding. I'm not even sure where to start," said Mila. "I mean, I don't have a job. All my things are still back in California."

"You don't worry 'bout that," said Irene, grabbing her hand. "I'm gonna send one of them boys to get your things. They ain't doin' nothin' except runnin' and workin' out."

"Grandma, that's called training," smiled Luke.

"And just how much trainin' do you need? You boys are already so big and muscular you can't find clothes to fit you. I need some time with these girls, so you boys do your business, and we'll see you at dinner." Irene scanned the room, staring up at her son, Miller. "Pierre? I heard you make that phone call. Don't you get yourself hurt, you promised Kari. And no more blowin' things up. You're too old for that."

"But Mama!"

"Don't but Mama, me. Cam? Eric? You boys might want to check in with Remy, Robbie, and the boys. I got a feelin' somethings 'bout to happen." She grabbed the two young women by the hand, pulling them toward the door. "Let's go. We got a lot to do."

The room was eerily silent as Fitch, Tim, Thomas, and Bron stared at the other men.

"Someone want to tell me what the hell that was?" asked Tim.

"That was Irene Robicheaux, Mama Irene, or just Irene," smirked Luke. "No ma'am or Mrs. She doesn't like that."

"How in the hell did she hear what they said?"

"It's a mystery to us all," growled Gaspar. "Code? Sly? Still no listening devices in here?" They both shook their heads. Only Noah let a small grin slip, smirking at the apparitions behind him.

"Alright, let's get this shit planned to perfection," said Cam, smiling at Thomas and Bron. "We don't want to miss the weddings of the month."

"Dad? This is a mission that you and the seniors can take part in and bring your lovely brides," smirked Luke. His father flipped him off but nodded.

"You think I won't take you up on that, but I damn sure will. In fact, why don't the 'seniors' and I talk to the wives and maybe spend a few extra days up in Napa while you young pups get some work done back here."

"Sounds good, Dad," laughed Luke.

"Alright, everyone. Time to get our shit together."

CHAPTER TWENTY-SIX

"How does she have a rack of wedding gowns in our size?" whispered May. Faith smiled at the young women.

"Mama Irene has a sixth sense when it comes to these things. When a woman first comes to Belle Fleur, it seems she's always connected in some way to one of the men. Irene knows right away whether it will last or not, and she begins planning."

"But, how?" asked Mila.

"She has a method of gathering information about you that even you don't see. She knows your size, your color preferences, everything. You'll see," smirked Grace.

"Alright now," said Mama Irene, holding two dresses in each arm. "I believe these will do well for choices. Mila? This will highlight that beautiful hourglass figure of yours without bein' too revealin'. May? These two are in ivory. I just thought it would look better with your skin and hair. I also called your mama and daddy. They'll be here this weekend for the wedding."

"Oh, my God," whispered May. "Did my mother flip out? She can be a bit overprotective."

"Not at all! She's a wonderful woman. We talked for an hour."

"You talked to my mother for an hour?" Mama Irene nodded, bustling out of the room again. "Holy hell, she's a witch, isn't she? She's some sort of shaman or something." The other women laughed, shaking their heads at the two women.

"You'll get used to it and love it, believe me. She has the uncanny ability of knowing when the kids are going to get sick, when someone is in trouble, or when one of us needs her. And believe me, that woman has been there for me more times than I can count," sniffed Grace.

“I don’t know if I can do this,” whispered Mila. “It’s all so fast. I mean, we’ve only known one another a few weeks. This can’t be real.”

“It’s time, Erin,” grinned Faith.

“Time?” chimed both women at the same time.

“Erin has given advice to almost every woman that’s married an RP man. When she wasn’t available, it was one of us or her daughter-in-law.”

“Well, I could use some advice right about now,” said Mila. “I’m seriously thinking of running.” She wasn’t serious, but she was damn sure close.

“Listen to me, these men, these men protect so fiercely, so devoutly it’s all-consuming. And they love the same way. All-consuming. It’s remarkable to watch and a blessing to be a part of it. If you want my advice, don’t question anything. Just let yourself feel. These are special men, and if you don’t mind me saying so… it will sound a bit conceited on my… on our part… but it takes special women to be with them.

“You two are very special, very extraordinary women. Bron and Thomas are new to the RP family, although Thomas was technically part of our family the moment Ian’s team saved him. We see everyone as family here. As a woman that grew up with no one, I can tell you that this is the most amazing feeling on the planet. Here. On this property, surrounded by these people, is a feeling like no other, and you are both so fortunate to be chosen by those two men.”

“Don’t run, Mila,” said Grace. “You’ll only be miserable. I can see it in your face. You love Bron, and more importantly, he loves you. The same for you, May. The minute you saw Thomas, you felt it, didn’t you?” May wiped the tears in her eyes and nodded.

"It was so strange," she whispered. "It was like this boulder hit me in the stomach. He's so tall and handsome, but he's also smart and kind, loving and tender. I've never had a man touch me the way he does or treat me the way he does."

"I feel the same about Bron," smiled Mila. "I hate myself for not telling him everything up front, but I let my past experiences with men blind me to a man who was open and honest, willing to hear me out. His ability to love and forgive is not something I've been used to, and I will always love him for that."

"And the sex?" grinned Faith. Mila blushed, looking down at her lap. "Honey, we talk openly around here. We support one another, cry on one another's shoulders, and slap the crap out of the husbands if they're being stupid." The woman all laughed, including Mila and May.

"We're a community," said Erin. "A community of powerful, intelligent, strong women who rely on one another when times are tough and when they're good. We don't get jealous or petty. We celebrate, raising our sisters, mothers, daughters, up!"

"Female friendship is a powerful thing," said Mama Irene coming into the room with an armful of wedding veils. Behind her, Matthew entered with a box of jewelry. "Thank you, my love." She kissed his cheek as he set the box down, and he winked at the girls.

"This is the woman you should aspire to be," he said, smiling at the girls. "You're already fine, strong, smart women, but it's your hearts that those boys fell in love with. Nurture his heart, and yours will be protected forever." Matthew kissed Irene once more and left the room.

"That's what I want to be married to in fifty years," smiled Mila.

"Honey, that's what we all want to be married to in fifty years," laughed Faith.

"But you are married to that," smiled Irene. "Every one of 'ya. You're married to some of the finest men God put on this planet. Now, a few of them are my own blood, but it doesn't make the rest of them any less loved. They're all exceptional men. Exceptional. And they're smart enough to marry exceptional women."

"God, I wish I'd been born into this family," Mila said with a pain-filled smile.

"God knew what he was doin', child. He brought you to us as soon as he could." Irene patted her cheek, smiling at the beautiful young women around her. She was proud of her boys, but she held reverence for her girls. Strong, beautiful, smart, independent women.

"Okay," smiled Irene, "now comes the fun part. Cake tasting. Let's go." As the women followed her downstairs, Mila turned to Grace and whispered.

"How does she already have cakes for us to taste?" Grace giggled, patting her shoulder.

"Honey, don't ask."

CHAPTER TWENTY-SEVEN

Critter Pine wasn't good at much, but he was very, very good at sneaking around. He was also good at killing people. The first thing he ever killed was Mrs. Mackenzie's cat. Damn thing scratched him, so he tied a rope around its neck and dragged it out back to the old well on his daddy's farm. Dangling the cat above the water, he watched it try to claw its way back up, then just dropped it.

That cat mewed for hours before finally drowning. It was exciting. No one knew it was him. He'd finally found something he was really good at. He'd killed a few more cats, a few dogs, a horse, and two of Mrs. Mackenzie's cows.

He left that Nebraska farm and just traveled, hoping to find work. There wasn't much available for a high school drop-out until he came across Rock Garvin. He was a graduate student working a dig in Montana. Some stupid shit about an ancient native tribe that Critter didn't understand. He wanted to get credit for something they were about to uncover, knowing it was there, yet unearthed.

Critter was happy to offer his services. At first, Rock didn't have the balls to kill someone. He just wanted them out of the way, so Critter put some nasty shit in the professor's water, and he was out for weeks with stomach parasites. Rock, back then Richard, got his first credit.

He basically kept him on retainer after that, flying him to sites all around the world to ensure he got the credit for the work. Now, he was standing about four hundred yards from the cave where some ancient Chinese guy was found. Critter didn't care and didn't want to know. He just wanted his money.

"Time to have some fun."

"Robbie? You see that boy tryin' to hide up there?" asked Remy.

"I'm not blind, Remy, and he's terrible at hide and seek. I see him. Colton and Buck down there with the doc?"

"Yep," grinned Remy. "What do you say you and I take a walk and give that dumbass a chance to sneak into the chamber?"

"I'll tell the Mongols to take a smoke break," grinned his brother.

Remy and Robbie walked toward the lake, talking about fishing and boating when they got back home to Louisiana. The Mongol soldiers liked the men right away and followed whatever instructions they gave them. Stepping to the far side of the opening, they took their smoke break, chatting away.

In the distance, Remy could see the man known as Critter, sneaking toward them. He casually walked to the cave opening, peering inside, and walked right in. Robbie raised a brow at his brother, shaking his head. Giving the man a minute to begin his descent, they followed while Colt and Buck readied for his arrival.

He stepped down from the bottom stair, watching the old man carefully taking notes on the tomb. Dr. Roth looked up, acting surprised.

"Who are you? What are you doing here? You have to leave, now."

"Old man, I'm not goin' anywhere," said Critter. "But you are. You're gonna have an unfortunate accident." Standing behind the coffin, Dr. Roth backed up as Colt and Buck Robicheaux stood, grinning at Critter. He tried to turn and run, but he ran straight into the brick wall chests of Remy and Robbie.

"Well, hello there, little man," smiled Robbie. "You tryin' to hurt our friend?"

"It's a mistake," he said, trying to back up.

"Nope. Uh, uh," grinned Remy. "Ain't no mistake about it. You tried to hurt our friend. Dr. Roth? You might want to head upstairs, sir."

Roth inched his way around the coffin, and as quickly as his old legs could carry him, he went up the steps.

"Who are you?" asked Critter.

"Oh, see that's not somethin' you need to know," smiled Buck. "But since I'm feelin' generous, we'll tell 'ya. See, we're cousins. Remy and Robbie are twin brothers. Me and Buck, we're just regular brothers, but we're all from the same family. The Robicheauxs."

"Am I supposed to know who that is?" Critter was scanning every corner of the cave, hoping for an exit, but the men had the stairs blocked.

"Nope. Nothin' real special about us," smiled Colt. "But there's somethin' really special about May Wong and Dr. Roth." Critter's eyes got big.

"I bet there's somethin' real special about the great Rock Garvin, too, ain't there?" laughed Robbie. "You two an item?"

"No! No, of course not," he proclaimed.

"Well, that's a shame," said Remy, shaking his head. "I bet he'd be the only one to cry over your grave."

"You can't kill me," smirked Critter. "The Mongols will arrest you."

"Yet you thought you could kill Dr. Roth? Now, that's some arrogance, boy," smirked Robbie. "I believe I've wasted enough breath. It's time for you to meet your maker, Bartholomew "Critter" Pine."

The other man's eyes grew wide, and he tried to make a dash for the stairs. Colt lifted a big boot, shoving him backwards against the stone wall. He was probably half their size with less than half their brainpower. Remy and Buck gripped his arms, pulling him back further into the darkness.

"No! No, you can't do this!" he screamed.

"You know, it was fascinating watching Dr. Roth explore this place. We didn't know it at first, but there's a whole other little bitty cave back here. There's nothin' in it. There's no exit. Don't know why, but we know it's perfect for you."

"No! You can't!"

The space was tight, so small it may have been made for a child. Doing Critter a favor, Buck punched his jaw so hard he knocked him out, then shoved him headfirst into the cramped, tiny opening. They'd taken his phone and his wallet, nothing on him identifiable. Lifting the two large concrete blocks, they cemented them in place.

"Helluva way to die," moaned Buck.

"Yep," nodded Robbie. "But I'm gonna bet God will agree he deserves it."

"God might not," smiled Remy, "but Aunt Irene would, and that's good enough for me."

CHAPTER TWENTY-EIGHT

"Critter! Damnit, call me the minute you get this message. We need to make sure that the situation is handled quickly. I'll be leaving San Francisco tomorrow morning and headed back. Call me!" screamed Garvin from the back seat of the town car. His outburst was met with an intense gaze by the gorilla in the front seat.

"What? Aren't you just supposed to be driving, not listening?" he snapped. Keith grinned at the man signing to him.

"Go fuck yourself, asshole."

"Oh, you're deaf. Whatever," he said, shaking his head.

As they neared the Japanese gardens, he noticed the spotlights swirling in the sky and people dressed in tuxedos and fine dresses glittering in the light. Beautiful women, their jewels hanging from their ears and necks. He didn't recognize any of his peers, but then again, he didn't really have any. This would be one more accolade to rub in their faces at the next conference.

He continued to look down at his phone every few seconds, obviously believing that Critter would call him back. Unfortunately, Critter no longer had cell service or any other service for that matter. The walls of the cave had been so thick you couldn't even hear him scream. A fitting end for a murderer and animal killer.

"Damn," he muttered as his phone rang. It was the network, no doubt asking where their money was. "Evan! Such a pleasure to hear from you."

"Cut the bullshit, Rock. You didn't find the site. Dr. Roth did. We want our money back, and we want it back now."

"Evan, you know these things take time. My money is in an offshore account that I can't access quite yet. I'll be sending it along soon, but just so you know, I'll be receiving an award this evening that will solidify the name Rock Garvin as the leading explorer and archaeologist on the planet. I'm sure you'll want me to do another dig somewhere soon."

He was met with silence, but he could hear the tapping of the other man's pen on his desk blotter. It was a nervous habit, one that annoyed the shit out of Garvin.

"What are you thinking?" asked Evan.

"Alexander the Great, or perhaps we try a sea adventure and look for the lost city of Atlantis," he said excitedly.

"Atlantis has been done to death, Garvin. Maybe Alexander, but the Egyptians and Turks pretty much have a hold on that. It would be incredibly difficult to get agreement and access to that information. Maybe. You're not exactly popular in that part of the world any longer. You were reckless on that last dig, and we lost sixteen men because of it. Sixteen men, Garvin. All because you couldn't wait for them to shore up those walls. The network had to pay their families."

"That wasn't my fault, Evan," he said, casually wiping a speck of lint from his pants. "Digs are dangerous, and those men weren't being careful. We had a deadline, Evan. A deadline that you and the network set, I might add."

"You were rushing them, Garvin. If we do this dig, and that's a big 'if,' someone will be supervising the workers other than you and reporting back to us directly."

"I'm in charge of the digs, Evan. I control the workers, the materials, everything. Me! No one else," yelled Garvin, sitting on the edge of his seat.

Keith slammed on his brakes, sending him flying forward into the back of the front seat. He shrugged, pointing to the car stopped in front of him.

"Shit! I've got a buffoon for a driver," he said, straightening himself back in the seat. "I am in charge of the dig sites, Evan, you know this. If you won't allow me to have full control, I can always go to another network." The man on the other end of the line was laughing so hard Keith could feel the vibrations coming from the phone.

"You're a fucking idiot. You're lucky that we decide to televise your bullshit explorations. No one else wants to. You're not an archaeologist, Rock. You're a wanna-be action movie star, and believe me, you'd fail miserably at that. I tell you what. I'm going to make a game-time call here. It's time we parted ways. This is no longer a fruitful relationship. You owe us the advance, Rock. Send that to us, and we'll call it even."

"Fine," he said, pursing his lips. "Fine! You'll be sorry about this, Evan! I'm the man everyone looks to for excitement, danger, and discovery."

"No, you're just a mediocre archaeologist with a cruel streak that is only rivaled by your immense ego."

The line went dead as they pulled into their parking spot in front of the gardens. A beautiful young woman walked toward the car as the driver stepped out. She was gorgeous with long, flowing black hair, exotic eyes that looked blue or perhaps violet. Her toned arms shimmered with the glow of light emitted by lanterns. He watched as she signed to the driver but ignored them as he tried Critter once again.

"Any trouble?" asked Susie.

"None, beautiful. That dress is stunning on you. Can I take it off with my teeth later?" grinned Keith.

"I'm not wearing anything underneath, so you won't have much to take off, but my answer is always yes, stud."

Keith desperately wanted to kiss her and take her behind the bushes, but in the distance, he saw her father and mother, her father staring at him with those eyes that said 'back the fuck off.' Susie might be his wife, but she would always be Trak's little girl. Susie laughed, seeing her father's glare, as Keith opened the door to the backseat.

"Dr. Garvin, it's such a pleasure to meet you," she said, smiling. "My name is Susie, and I'm here to make sure you get to where you should be."

"Well," he grinned, looking her up and down, "things are definitely looking up."

"Dr. Garvin, I'm a married woman," she giggled, winking to Keith.

"He's a lucky man, but I'm sure he wouldn't mind you having a little fun tonight." Garvin attempted to reach for her, hopefully, to snake an arm around her waist, but she expertly slid to the side, avoiding his touch.

"Oh, I'm going to have a lot of fun tonight, believe me," she smiled. "Right this way."

Susie led him down the path and between the trees to a flat green space with lanterns hanging above the tables and chairs. Heaters were placed around the garden to help ward off the typical San Francisco chill. Leading him to a large table at the front of the garden, she pointed to his chair, and he took his seat, smiling at the wiggling ass of the beautiful woman.

Looking up, he noticed his chauffeur staring at him, and he simply nodded at him.

“Dr. Garvin?” said Miller, standing straight and tall in his tuxedo. Kari was linked to his arm, her off-white beaded gown revealing a body that a woman her age shouldn’t have. Her dark hair was twisted high on her head, exposing her beautiful neck and full breasts.

“Yes,” he smiled, staring at Kari as he took Miller’s hand. Miller squeezed a little harder than necessary, and the man actually said ouch.

“My apologies, I don’t know my own strength sometimes. I’m Peter Webster. We spoke on the phone.”

“Oh, yes, of course. Very nice to meet you. When will this get started?” he asked. He attempted to get up but felt as though something was holding him down. Miller held up a hand, assuring him it was fine to stay seated.

“Soon enough, Dr. Garvin,” smiled Miller. “We have a few speakers here for you first. Admirers of your work that would like to say a few words. After all, this evening could not be possible without your contributions.”

“Lovely,” he said, nodding. Then he frowned, wondering who it could be. He didn’t have a lot of admirers or friends in his industry. Most were so jealous they separated themselves from him. It could be some young students he’d recently spoken to, although that might end poorly considering he took two of the grad students back to his hotel.

Miller stepped up to the dais, and Garvin glanced over both shoulders, seeing the resplendent vision of gorgeous women and some men that appeared attractive behind him. He never liked there to be men that competed for the spotlight with him. His face was made for television. Fine chiseled features, blonde hair, thick and lustrous. If other men were around, it showed that he wasn’t as big as television made him appear.

"Ladies and gentlemen, thank you for coming this evening to the trial and execution of Richard Geller, better known as Rock Garvin."

Garvin's face paled, the saliva gone from his mouth. He had a sudden urge to run to the bathroom, but he couldn't get out of his seat. He couldn't move. He was trying, but his clothing was literally stuck to the chair.

"Yea, no." Miller looked at the man shaking his head. "That's industrial cement with an additional compound of our own making. If you attempt to move, your clothes will rip off your body, and most likely, take some of your skin with it. And that gorgeous young woman you were drooling over is the wife of your so-called chauffeur, and he's gonna kick your ass. Most likely not before I do, though. You see, this vision is my wife."

"What the hell is happening?" he murmured. He felt the hot breath against his ear and stilled.

"What's the matter, Richard? Don't you like being the center of attention any longer?" asked May.

"May? May, help me, honey. You know we're still good for one another. Help me get away. These men are crazy."

"Crazy? No, these men are amazing, and I'm going to marry one of these men. He is everything you are not, including a genius."

"That's me, dumbass," said Thomas, wrapping a big arm around May's waist. Garvin squirmed, trying to break free from his chair, but it was no use.

"What do you want?" he said, staring at Miller. Four more men stepped in front of him, and he swallowed, staring up at them. Cam, Luke, Eric, and Bron frowned at him.

"You killed two people in this city not all that long ago," said Bron. "Two people who deserved to live. One of them was my ex-wife."

"No," he said, shaking his head. He saw a face he recognized, and panic began to rise in his throat. "No, I didn't kill them. That crazy man, Critter, he killed them. Tim! Tim, tell them!"

"You ordered everything, including the kill on Dr. Roth. In fact," he said, reaching into his pocket, "you gave me this check for helping to convince Mike to gather that information for you. I regret that, and I'm glad I was able to tell Mike to hide the originals. I'm sad I didn't protect him after that, but honestly, I never believed you were crazy enough to kill him."

"This is a mistake! This is all Critter."

"We don't have to worry about him any longer," smiled Eric. "He's buried with the secrets of his sins. He'll have an eternity to work that out."

"Oh, God. You're crazy. You're all crazy!" he yelled.

Suddenly there were fifty men standing around his table. As each row stood behind the other, they seemed to get taller and bigger. May Wong stood with her protector, another woman standing beside her, holding her hand.

"Mike Hartfeld was my brother. Lora was my roommate, and they were in love. They obviously knew what a sleazeball you were because they left me the original documents and took the fakes with them. They knew you were coming for them and knew you would probably have them killed, and for some reason, they let you come. You did the only thing you knew you could do. Mike was a Marine, and you would have never beat him face-to-face, so you sent in your slimy hitman to poison them. I have to believe that both of them had a change of heart at the end."

"No," he growled. "No, Hartfeld was an idiot."

"He was a good man. A good Marine," said Bron. "He knew enough to know that whatever you were doing with the find would be bad. So, we beat you to it. May actually found the site, but she gave the credit to Dr. Roth. Pretty nice of her if you ask me."

"I didn't ask you," seethed Garvin.

"Boy, you got balls, I'll give you that," laughed Bron. "What did the North Koreans and the Russians offer you for the weapon? I bet it was a lot, wasn't it?" The men all nodded, smiling at Garvin as cold sweat poured down his face.

"I'm going to guess," said May, "because you're cocky and self-assured, when you have no right to be, that you took a deposit from both of them, didn't you?"

"May, please, you have to help me. We were good together, baby. Don't you remember?" he pleaded. "This man can't compare to me."

"Oh, my God," she laughed, doubling over, giggling as Mila laughed with her. Garvin's face froze, staring at the two women. "You? You, Richard, do not compare even a little to this man. This man is honest, true, sexy, and hot as hell in bed."

"You go, Thomas!" yelled Cruz. Thomas blushed, shrugging his shoulders.

"You aren't a man, Richard. You're a pathetic, weak piece of shit who steals from others, taking credit for their work. You don't deserve to breathe the same air as any of these men."

"May, honey, look, you were sick, and I made that find, and things just started to roll. I didn't mean to take all the credit. It just happened. The others, the others, weren't ready to handle the fame that came with such high-stakes digs. I was helping them."

"Helping them? By taking the credit for their work? By killing people when you didn't get your way? You're nothing but a teeny, tiny man with an even smaller penis," said May.

"Fuck you!" he screamed. "You're nothing but a two-bit whore pretending to be an archaeologist."

He didn't see it coming, but he damn sure felt it. The thrust of Thomas's fist into his face sent his chair backwards. Then he felt a heeled foot in his groin and gasped, staring up at Mila.

"Did you get all of that?" Mila asked someone off to the left.

"We got it," said Evan. "I do believe the good doctor is going to have one last hit show."

"No! No, you can't do this to me! They'll kill me! They'll come for me and kill me!" he screamed. Three police officers lifted the chair, literally tossing him into the back of the police van.

"Thank you for coming out, Evan," said May.

"It's my pleasure, honey. I always suspected he stole that dig from you, but we couldn't prove it, and unfortunately, ratings win in my world. He won't be working on any network again unless it's a prison network."

"He won't make it that far," said Bron, glowering at Garvin. "He's right. The North Koreans and the Russians will come for him if he took money from them."

"Well, I'd say that's justice," smiled Evan, walking toward the waiting car. Thomas kissed the top of May's head, smiling down at her.

"You did great, baby."

"So, did you. How's the hand?" He opened it and closed it, grinning at her.

"Works just fine. Of course, if you have a medical remedy that will make it better, I say we make use of the hotel room here."

"Let's go, Dr. Bradshaw."

"Following you, Dr. Wong."

Mila clung to Bron, worried that he might decide this was the end. He could sense it in her body posture, the way she was afraid to let go of him. Taking her hand, he pulled her to the side where they could speak privately.

"Mila, baby, I'm not going anywhere, and neither are you. I think May and Thomas have the right idea. We'll use that big hotel suite tonight and go back to Belle Fleur in the morning. We have a wedding this weekend."

Mila nodded, tears streaming down her face as she hugged him.

"Aw, baby, you're killin' me here," said Bron. "We're going to have a beautiful life together, Mila. You found Mike and Lora's killer, and he's going to be spending the rest of his life in prison." She nodded, wiping her eyes.

"I don't have anyone to walk me down the aisle. May offered her father up to me, but it seems wrong. They should share their moment alone."

"Baby girl, look around you. There are dozens of men you could ask to walk you down the aisle. Any one of them would do that for you."

"Really?" Bron nodded, giving her a sexy smirk. She pushed away from him, walking toward Cam, Luke, and Eric. "Hi."

"Hi, Mila," said Cam. "Everything okay, honey?"

"No. I mean, yes, but I have something to ask you."

"Me?" squawked Cam.

"Yes," she smiled. "My adoptive parents are no longer alive, Cam. If Mike were alive, I'd ask him, but, well, I need someone to walk me down the aisle this weekend." Cam was stunned. Absolutely stunned.

"Me?" he repeated. Mila laughed.

"Yes, you. You gave me some pretty good pep talks these last few weeks, Cam. You're about Mike's age, so it seems right. Will you? I mean, will you walk me down the aisle?"

"Oh, honey," said Cam, pulling her in for a brotherly hug, "of course, I will! I'd be damn proud." Mila kissed his cheek, walking back to Bron. Eric nudged him, grinning.

"You know, I do believe the seniors started out this way," laughed Eric. "My father-in-law walked Erin down the aisle. Wilson walked Lauren down the aisle, and so on, and so on." Cam and Luke both nodded, laughing.

"I guess I need to make sure my tux and uniform are pressed," he chuckled. He smiled as Kate, his beautiful wife, hugged Mila. "If you gentlemen will excuse me. I do believe I have a hotel room for an entire night, along with my beautiful bride. I'll see you in the morning."

Tim walked up to Eric and Luke, frowning. He swallowed, looking as though he were going to cry.

"What now?" he asked.

"We promised you we would help with your divorce proceedings, Tim, and we will. There are some things that have to be taken care of with the SEALs before we can make any promises on our end." Luke gripped his shoulder, squeezing hard.

"I understand. Should I head back to Pendleton and wait?" he asked.

"No," said Eric. "You can come back with us. It would be better if we have you close by and handle things quickly as they arise. As you know, Tim, it will be whether or not the SEALs and Pendleton think you should be implicated in Mike's death. You didn't steal that information, but you used Mike's weakness to get him to do it."

"I know," he said, nodding. Eric gripped his neck with one big bear paw and flashed his sweet smile.

"Come on, brother. Let's go home."

CHAPTER TWENTY-NINE

It didn't take long for Catherine Pearson to realize she was in deep shit. Once Kari and the legal team gave the proof that Alexis wasn't Tim's child, she started to back-peddle. They were able to get her to agree to the divorce, taking only half of Tim's pension. It still stung, but he was free of that burden but would never see the little girl he believed was his daughter again.

As for his future, it was now in the hands of the SEALs, Pendleton, and JAG. He would have a long row to hoe, most likely avoiding any prison time, but he could lose some of his benefits. It seemed, in their infinite wisdom, the Marines determined that Mike was capable of making his own decisions and should not have been coerced by Tim. They did not want to admit that they'd missed the diagnosis of his learning challenges.

He'd left the previous day, headed back to face the music. Kari, Kat, Katrina, and Georgie assured him they would help him. Tim Pearson might be worth saving.

The Wongs seemed to fit right in with the Robicheaux family. Mrs. Wong thought that Irene was the most amazing woman on the planet, and everyone agreed with her. As the reception kicked off with dancing and food, Thomas and May sat at the table with Bron and Mila.

"Who is that man my aunt is dancing with?" asked May. Thomas and Bron looked across the dance floor and grinned.

"I'll be damned," smirked Bron. "That's former Navy SEAL and Senator Michael Bodwick. He's been here for a few years now, but I don't think he's dated anyone." Bron noticed his friend Fitch leaning against a tree, holding the neck of a beer bottle, and frowned.

Fitch stared at the couples dancing around the floor, sipping the beer in his hand. He'd had two weddings of his own, both ending disastrously. More his fault than theirs. He'd chosen the wrong women both times, letting his dick lead his decision-making process.

A young Marine, feeling invincible, Debbie approached him in a bar with her double-D fake breasts hanging out of a bikini top, and he nearly melted. They were married two weeks later and fucking like rabbits in heat. As he was about to head out for another deployment, she suggested they invite her friend, Tamara, to join them for a little fun.

Fitch thought nothing of it. Hell, it was every man's fantasy to have two women at once. He thought if she was cool with it, so was he. The three of them enjoyed some highly aerobic and gymnastic-like exercises for the entire night. Two nights later, Debbie called to say she was working late, and Tamara suddenly popped by.

He shook his head. Young and dumb. He fucked her like a starving man attacks a buffet, and left for deployment the next day. He never thought Tamara would tell Debbie. He came home to divorce papers, an empty apartment, and Tamara offering herself up to him. What's a young, horny man to do? Her. That's what he did. He did her.

Except she wasn't any different than his ex-wife. She wanted to be the wife of a Marine without all the deployments and the lack of pay. Within three months, they were fighting like cats and dogs, and she was racking up credit card debt. It took him three years to finalize the divorce and get his credit back to where it needed to be.

Looking at Bron and Mila, he knew that they were different. First of all, they were old enough to know the difference between love and lust. Second, they were mature enough to understand what had to happen for a marriage to be successful. And third, they just looked blissfully, fucking happy. He knew for a fact that he never had that look on his face with either one of his wives.

He felt the nudge of an arm and turned to see Bron.

"You okay, brother?" he asked.

"I'm good, man. Commiserating on my miserable marriage mistakes."

"I'm not sure they were marriage mistakes. I think they were more relationship mistakes," smirked Bron. "You were young, Fitch. Like the rest of us, you mistook fucking for loving."

"The rest of you didn't fuck and marry. You fucked and left. I should have learned that lesson after the first woman, but I didn't. I'm not sure this happily ever after bullshit will ever happen to me."

"Oh, man," said Bron, shaking his head. "You just assured yourself that it will happen. Speak those words on this property with that little, tiny woman over there anywhere near you, and you will be the next man down the aisle." Bron laughed all the way to his bride, who was waiting for him on the dance floor.

"Shit," muttered Fitch.

CHAPTER THIRTY

While Bron and Mila decided on a honeymoon to Greece, Thomas and May took off to Hong Kong to visit her extended family. The Monday morning meeting was a little quieter but still filled the auditorium with the men of the team.

"We've got some small jobs happening right now, but nothing huge. Honestly, it's time we had a bit of a break. Fitch? New man and all that, brother. We've been asked by a friend of Grandma's to find her granddaughter."

"She was kidnapped?" asked Fitch.

"No, we think she's hiding. Miss Ruby owns a few strip clubs and apparel shops," grinned Cam. "She's also a wonderful woman. She contributes to the community and is always there lending a hand when someone needs it. She and Mama Irene are great friends."

"Okay, but why is the granddaughter hiding?" asked Fitch.

"Miss Ruby believes she saw something that she shouldn't have. Her granddaughter wouldn't tell her everything over the phone, just that she saw her boss do something, and now she believes she's in danger."

"Why didn't she call the police?" asked Fitch.

"She's in Mexico." The groans and heads shaking around the room told Fitch what he already knew. The corruption by the Mexican police, particularly in smaller communities, was notorious.

"Where in Mexico?"

"The last time Miss Ruby spoke with her, she was the night manager at a hotel, La Casa de las Lunas. She was doing some graduate work on ancient Mayan cultures and worked part-time at a museum outside of Chichén Itzá."

"This sounds like May's expertise, not mine."

"This isn't about the museum," said Luke. "It's about her hiding from whoever her boss is. Now, we're not sure if it was her boss at the museum or her boss at the hotel. All we know is that this young woman called for help, and we're going to help her. We don't want it to appear as if we're sending an entire team down there, but we will have Cruz, Razor, and Jax, along with their wives, on a cruise ship, sitting just off Cancun.

"They're all familiar with the area and speak Spanish fluently, just like you." Fitch nodded. "We've got a few pictures of the girl. Ace?" Ace nodded, connecting his computer to the screen.

"These are a few years old, but her grandmother doesn't think she's changed much. She hasn't been home in about two years." Fitch looked at the photos of a young woman with short hair styled around her ears. Her hair was a light brown, her eyes also light brown. She appeared to have a mild case of acne, but if the photo was taken a few years ago, that might be gone.

"Her details are in the information I sent to you," said Ace. "She's about five-nine. Her grandmother thinks she's about one-sixty."

"If we have to run, is she in good enough shape to run through that jungle?" asked Fitch.

"Brother, I don't know," said Luke. "Evie will fly you into Cancun. From there, rent a car. Take all the weapons you can carry, Fitch. If you get stopped, even if it's the federales, kill first, ask questions later."

“I’ll head out now,” he said, nodding at the group. Mama Irene walked into the room, smiling up at Fitch. She handed him a brown paper bag with sandwiches and cookies, kissing his cheek.

“Bring my friend’s granddaughter home, baby.”

“I will, Mama Irene, I promise,” he smiled, opening the bag. “I don’t think I’ve ever been given a lunch to carry with me for a mission.”

“First time for everything, baby.” She patted his cheek and followed him out of the office building. Evie was waiting at the jeep to head to the helipad. He set the sack in the car, telling Evie he needed to grab his go-bag and a few weapons. As he started to walk away, he turned back to Irene.

“Something on your mind, Patrick?” she asked, using his first name.

“It’s actually been weighing on my mind for a few days, Mama Irene. As you know, I was rather reckless in my youth. Married twice. Divorced Twice.” She nodded. “I was just wondering, how will I know if it’s real, Mama Irene? I thought it was real before and was most definitely wrong both times.”

“Oh, honey, when it’s real, you don’t just feel it in your private parts,” she grinned. “You feel it all over your body. Your heart stops, your head spins, your hands sweat. Your moods are up and down. Sometimes, your logic is just out the window. When it’s real, you know that life will never be the same as you know it.” Fitch grinned at the old woman, bending to kiss her cheek.

A few minutes later, he returned and took off down the road with Evie. Irene stood watching him, George and Julia behind her. Martha, Joseph, Franklin, Grip, Tony, and Anthony behind them.

“This won’t be easy for him,” said Julia.

“It never is,” scoffed George. “These boys, they can handle danger, but anything else, they struggle.”

"He'll do alright," said Grip. "I'll make sure."

Julia turned to face her partners in crime, as well as her companion ghosts.

"I love you, all. You do know that, right?"

"We know, baby," said Irene. "We love you too."

EXCERPT from FITCH

Sending text messages back and forth to an eighty-five-year-old woman was not how Fitch was used to operating a mission. This should have been an easy extraction, but every time he went to a location where Carsen Benoit was supposed to meet him, she didn't show. Now, he was standing at the ancient steps of the Mayan ruins near the hotel, scanning the crowds for her.

He felt his phone vibrate in his pocket and stared at the message on the screen.

She says she's inside the second pyramid at the top of the stairs.

"Fuck me," he mumbled. The cramped space was not made for a man as wide as he was. He was six-feet-two, but his two hundred and thirty pounds of muscle was wide and unyielding.

Several people squeezed by him as he sucked in his chest and flattened his body to the wall. He kept moving up the stairs, finally coming to a small open chamber. There was a young couple with a little boy who didn't seem to give a shit that he was inside a pyramid. On the other side were two men, and in the corner was a woman with great legs, but that's all he could see.

Behind him, he heard shuffling on the stairs, so he moved further into the chamber, giving the new arrivals more space. The young woman in front of him turned and gasped. Gripping his t-shirt, she pulled him toward her, slamming her mouth against his. She laced her fingers through his hair, her tongue dancing with his.

At first, Fitch wanted to push back. But what kind of dumbass would do that? She was fucking hot, and this woman knew how to kiss. He gripped her hips, pulling her tighter to his body as she just kept exploring, forcing him to push her against the pyramid wall. Behind him, he heard a bit of commotion but ignored it.

A few moments later, she pulled back, staring up at him.

"Well, hello to you, too," he grinned.

"You can let me go now," she said, staring daggers at him.

"You grabbed me, sweetheart." He held up his hands as she looked behind him. Seeing the coast was clear.

"I grabbed you because those are the men that are after me. Is this how you treat all the women you rescue?" she seethed.

"Wh-what? Fuck. You're Carsen Benoit," he whispered. "You don't look like your photo."

"That's because my grandmother insists on using my college graduation photo. You're a great kisser, by the way."

"Thanks. So are you." She stared at him, waiting for him to make the next move. He slowly reached for her, and she frowned.

"What the fuck are you doing? Are we getting out of here or what?" She headed toward the stairs, and Fitch rolled his eyes, pissed at himself.

"Right. Bad guys."

Note to Readers

Much of what I put in this book about Genghis Kahn is fact. There is also a great deal that I took liberties with. His tomb has never been found, but it is believed to be in the mountain region mentioned. There is no evidence of a weapon or treasure buried with him, and the idea of a casket similar to those of the pharaohs of Egypt seems a stretch. The bits of his conquests are correct. Rumors have swirled that a woman killed him in his bed with a knife, but again, we have no proof of that.

He is a fascinating character in history and one that historians are on opposite sides of the spectrum as to his status as hero or villain. I was fortunate enough to stand on the Great Wall and look at Mongolia in the distance. It was humbling, to say the least.

The book – Secret History of the Mongols – is real, and if you love history, it's worth the read.

SERIES AND FAMILY GUIDE

(#) Book in Series	*Name of Series*	Character Name	Spouse	Child	Child's Spouse
1	***Reaper Security***	Joe "Nine" Dougall	Erin Richards	Joy Elizabeth "Ellie"	Jackson "Jax" Diaz
				Cameron	Kate Robicheaux
2	***Reaper Security***	Joseph "Trak" Redhawk	Lauren Owens	Sophia	Eric Bongard
				Suzette	Keith Robicheaux
				Nathan	Katrina Santos
				Joseph	Julia Anderson
3	***Reaper Security***	Billy Joe "Tailor" Bongard	Cholena "Lena" Blackwood	Eric	Sophia Ann Redhawk
4	***Reaper Security***	Dan "Wilson" Anderson	Sara MacMillan	Paige	Ryan Holden Robicheaux
				Julia	Joseph Redhawk
5	***Reaper Security***	Luke "Angel" Jordan	Mary Fitzhugh	Marc (Luke)	Ela Wolfkill
				Georgianna	Carl Robicheaux
				Wesley	Virginia Robicheaux
6	***Reaper Security***	Peter "Miller" Robicheaux	Kari LeBlanc	Frank Gaspar	Lane Quinn
7	***Reaper Security***	Rachelle Robicheaux	Frank "Mac" MacMillan	Danielle (Dani) Marie	Dev Parker
8	***Reaper Security***	Adele Robicheaux	Clay Duffy		
9	***Reaper Security***	Gabriel Robicheaux	Tory Gibson		
9	***Reaper Security***	John "Gibbie" Gibson	Dhara	Dalton	Calla Michaels
9	***Reaper Security***	Antoine Robicheaux	Ella Stanton	Ryan Holden Robicheaux	Paige Anderson
9	***Reaper Security***	Gaspar Robicheaux	Alexandra Minsky	Luke	Ajei Blackwood
				Carl	Georgianna Jordan
				Ben	Harper Miller
				Adam	Jane Wolfkill
	Steel Patriots			Violet	Striker Michaels
6	***Reaper Patriots***			Lucy	Alex "Sniff" Mullins
10	***Reaper Security***	William "Bull" Stone	Lily Bennett		
11	***Reaper Security***	Luc Robicheaux	Montana Divide		
12	***Reaper Security***	Raphael Robicheaux	Savannah O'Reilly	Ian Luke	Aspen Bodwick
				Katherine Gray "Kate"	Cameron Dougall
		Doug Graham	*Deceased partner – Grip* Current partner – Miguel Santos		
13	***Reaper Security***	Jasper "Jazz" Divide	Gray Vanzant	Virginia	Wes Jordan
14	***Reaper Security***	Baptiste Robicheaux	Rose Ellis	Elizabeth Irene "Liz"	Kiel Wolfkill
14	***Reaper Security***	Alec Robicheaux	Lissa Duncan	Keith	Susie Redhawk

(#) Book in Series	*Name of Series*	**Character Name**	**Spouse**	**Child**	**Child's Spouse**
15	***Reaper Security***	Stone Roberts	Bronwyn Ross		
16	***Reaper Security***	Suzette Robicheaux	Sylvester "Sly" DiMarco		
16	***Reaper Security***	Max Neill	Riley Corbett	CC	
17	***Reaper Security***	Titus Quinn	Olivia Baine	Lane	Frank Robicheaux
				Dominic	Leightyn Dooley
18	***Reaper Security***	Axel Doyle	Cait Brennan	Corey	
		Vince Martin	Ally Lawrence	Christian Martin	
19	***Reaper Security***	Phoenix Keogh	Raven Foster		
	Reaper Security	Crow Foster			
19	***Reaper Security***	Wesley "Pigsty" O'Neal	Aasira "Sira" Al Aman		
20	***Reaper Security***	Zeke Wolfkill	Noelle Hart	Ezekiel ('Kiel)	Liz Divide
				Jane	Adam Robicheaux
20	***Reaper Security***	Elias Haggerty	Janie Granier		
20	***Reaper Security***	Russell "RJ" Jones	Celia Granier		
	Reaper Security	Chad Taylor			
	Reaper Security	Woody "Doc" Fine			
	Reaper Security	(d) Tony Parks			
	Reaper Security	(d) Alan Haley			
	Reaper Security	Michael Bodwick		Aspen	Ian Robicheaux
	Reaper Security	Miguel Santos	Doug	Katrina	Nathan Redhawk
	Reaper Security	Luke Robicheaux	Ajei Blackwood	Garrett	
1	***My Seal Boys***	Ian Shepard	Faith Gallagher	Kelsey Gallagher	Noa Lim
2	***My Seal Boys***	Noa Lim	Kelsey Gallagher		
3	***My Seal Boys***	Dave Carter	Ani Lim		
4	***My Seal Boys***	Lars Merrick	Jessica Fisher		
5	***My Seal Boys***	Trevor Banks	Ashley Dalton		
5	***My Seal Boys***	John Cruz	Camille Robicheaux		
6	***My Seal Boys***	Alec "Fitz" Fitzhenry	Zoe Myers		
7	***My Seal Boys***	Chris Paul	Elizabeth Broussard		
8	***My Seal Boys***	Luke O'Hara	Lucia Salvado		
8	***My Seal Boys***	Rory Baine	Piper Colley		
	My Seal Boys	(d) Anthony Garcia			
	My Seal Boys	Eric & Anna Tanner			
1	***Steel Patriots MC***	Eric "Ghost" Stanton	Grace Easton	(d) Faith & Hope	
				Jack Tyran "JT"	

(#) Book in Series	*Name of Series*	Character Name	Spouse	Child	Child's Spouse
				Eric Ryan	
2	***Steel Patriots MC***	Jack "Doc" Harris	Aubrey "Bree" Collins	Eva Irene	
3	***Steel Patriots MC***	Wade "Whiskey" English	Katrina Krevnyv	Juliette Rose	
4	***Steel Patriots MC***	Quincy "Zulu" Slater	Gabrielle London	Wade Eric	
				Tyler Gunner	
5	***Steel Patriots MC***	Gunner Michaels	Darby Greer	Calla	Dalton Gibson
6	***Steel Patriots MC***	Tyler "Tango" Green	Taylor Holland	Chase Maxwell	
7	***Steel Patriots MC***	Diego "Razor" Salcedo	Isabella "Bella" Castro		
8	***Steel Patriots MC***	Alex "Ace" Mills	Charlotte "CC Robat" Tabor	Alexander John "AJ"	
9	***Steel Patriots MC***	Tyran "Eagle" O'Neal	Tinley Oakley	Tyran Eagle	
				Hawk Gunner	
				Benjamin Scott	
9	***Steel Patriots MC***	Ryan "Hawk" O'Neal	Keegan Oakley		
10	***Steel Patriots MC***	Scott "Skull" Crawford	Willa Ross (deceased) Avery O'Connor	Mathew Scott	
				Kevin Alexander	
11	***Steel Patriots MC***	Benjamin "Blade" LeBlanc	Suzette Doiron	Benjamin Alfonse	
12	***Steel Patriots MC***	Noah Anders	Tru Blanchard	William Rush	
13	***Steel Patriots MC***	Tristan Evers	Emma Colvin	Hannah Ivana	
14	***Steel Patriots MC***	Ivan Pechkin	Sophia Lord	William	
				Benjamin	
				Celeste	
				Cassidy	
				Carrie	
15	***Steel Patriots MC***	Griffin "Griff" James	Amanda Nettles		
16	***Steel Patriots MC***	Bryce Nolan	Ivy Brooks		
17	***Steel Patriots MC***	Kingston Miles	Claire Evers		
18	***Steel Patriots MC***	Grant Zimmerman	Everly "Evie" Johnson		
	Steel Patriots MC	Molly Walker	Asia	boy	
	Steel Patriots MC	George Robert Williamson	Mary		
	Steel Patriots MC	(d) Axel "Axe" Mains	(d) Decker "Ice" McManus		
	Steel Patriots MC	James Scarlutti			
	Steel Patriots MC	Chen Wu		Choi Wu	
	Steel Patriots MC	Ian Laughlin			
	Steel Patriots MC	Conor Laughlin			

(#) Book in Series	*Name of Series*	**Character Name**	**Spouse**	**Child**	**Child's Spouse**
	Steel Patriots MC	Vincent Scalia		(d) Isabella	
1	***Reaper-Patriots***	Dexter Lock	Marie Robicheaux		
2	***Reaper-Patriots***	Jean Robicheaux	Rose "Ro" Evers		
3	***Reaper-Patriots***	Jackson "Jax" Diaz	Joy "Ellie" Dougall		
4	***Reaper-Patriots***	Hunter Michaels	Megan Scott		
5	***Reaper-Patriots***	Carl Robicheaux	Penelope Georgianna "Georgie" Jordan		
6	***Reaper-Patriots***	Alex "Sniff" Mullins	Lucy Robicheaux	Caroline Willa	
7	***Reaper-Patriots***	Cameron "Cam" Dougall	Kate Robicheaux	Ian William	
8	***Reaper-Patriots***	Keith Robicheaux	Suzette "Susie" Redhawk	Joseph Alec Keith (JAK)	
9	***Reaper-Patriots***	Eric Bongard	Sophia Ann Redhawk	Billy Joseph	
10	***Reaper-Patriots***	Joseph Redhawk	Julia Anderson	Joseph Billy (JB)	
				Tobias Franklin	
11	***Reaper-Patriots***	Ryan Robicheaux (Holden)	Paige Anderson	Dan Antoine	
12	***Reaper-Patriots***	Nathan Redhawk	Katrina Santos	Nathan Luke	
				Michael Douglas	
13	***Reaper-Patriots***	Ben Robicheaux	Harper Miller		
14	***Reaper-Patriots***	Sean Liffey	Shay Miller		
15	***Reaper-Patriots***	Ezekiel 'Kiel' Wolfkill	Elizabeth 'Liz' Robicheaux	Everett Baptiste	
				Eastman Matthew	
				Ethan Ezekiel	
16	***Reaper-Patriots***	Ian Robicheaux	Aspen Bodwick		
17	***Reaper-Patriots***	Adam Robicheaux	Jane Wolfkill		
18	***Reaper-Patriots***	Marc Jordan	Ela Wolfkill		
19	***Reaper-Patriots***	Wes Jordan	Virginia Divide	Patrick Jasper	
				Christopher Luke	
				Sadie Allison	
20	***Reaper-Patriots***	Aiden Wagner	Brit Elig		
21	***Reaper-Patriots***	Devin Parker	Danielle 'Dani' MacMillan		
22	***Reaper-Patriots***	Dalton Gibson	Calla Michaels		
23	***Reaper-Patriots***	Frank Robicheaux	Lane Quinn		
24	***Reaper-Patriots***	Hirohito Tanaka	Winter Cole		
25	***Reaper-Patriots***	Dominic 'Dom' Quinn	Leightyn Dooley	(preg)	

OTHER BOOKS BY MARY KENNEDY YOU MIGHT ENJOY!

REAPER Security Series

Erin's' Hero
Lauren's Warrior
Lena's' Mountain
Sara's' Chance
Mary's Angel
Kari's Gargoyle
Rachelle's Savior
Adele's Heart
Tori's' Secret
Finding Lily
Montana Rules
Savannah Rain
Gray Skies
My First Choice
Three Wishes
Second Chances
One Day at a Time
When You Least Expect It
Missing Hearts
Trail of Love

My SEAL Boys (connections to the REAPER Series)

Ian
Noa
Carter
Lars
Trevor
Fitz
Chris
O'Hara

Steel Patriots MC Series

Ghost – Book One
Doc – Book Two
Whiskey – Book Three
Zulu – Book Four
Gunner – Book Five
Tango – Book Six
Razor – Book Seven
Ace – Book Eight
Hawk & Eagle – Book Nine
Skull – Book Ten
Blade – Book Eleven
Noah – Book Twelve
Tristan – Book Thirteen
Ivan – Book Fourteen
Griff – Book Fifteen

Steel Patriots MC Series (continued)

Bryce – Book Sixteen
King – Book Seventeen
Grant – Book Eighteen
Striker – Book Nineteen

REAPER-Patriots Series

Dex – Book One
Jean – Book Two
Jax – Book Three
Hunter – Book Four
Carl – Book Five
Sniff – Book Six
Cam – Book Seven
Keith – Book Eight
Eric – Book Nine
Joseph – Book Ten
Ryan – Book Eleven
Nathan – Book Twelve
Ben – Book Thirteen
Sean – Book Fourteen
Kiel – Book Fifteen
Ian – Book Sixteen
Adam – Book Seventeen
Marc – Book Eighteen
Wes – Book Nineteen
Aiden – Book Twenty
Parker – Book Twenty-one
Dalton – Book Twenty-two
Frank – Book Twenty-three
Hiro – Book Twenty-four
Dom – Book Twenty-five

REAPER-Patriots Christmas: Do You Believe?

Strange Gifts Series

Dark Visions
Dark Medicine
Dark Flame

ABOUT THE AUTHOR

Mary Kennedy is the mother of two adult children, has an amazing son-in-law, and is grandmother to two beautiful grandsons. She works full-time at a job she loves, and writing is her creative outlet. She lives in Texas and enjoys traveling, reading, and cooking. Her passion for assisting veterans and veteran causes comes from a strong military family background. Mary loves to hear from her readers and encourages them to join her mailing list, as she'll keep you up-to-date on new releases at https://insatiableink.squarespace.com. You can also join her Facebook page at Insatiable Ink.

Dear Readers,

I love hearing from you and encourage you to visit my website insatiableink.squarespace.com. Let me know your thoughts and ideas on new books or expanding on characters. It's also a safe space to give your own feelings, like those of the characters. I love reading about how you relate to the stories because as we all know, there's a little of each of them within us.

I look forward to hearing from you and hope you enjoy other books in my collections.

Explore... and enjoy!

Printed in Great Britain
by Amazon

10529155R00112